USA Today BESTSELLING AUTHOR

Dale Mayer

TERK'S GUARDIANS
RADAR 01

RADAR: TERK'S GUARDIANS, BOOK 1
Beverly Dale Mayer
Valley Publishing Ltd.

ISBN-13: 978-1-773367-92-7
Print Edition

Books in This Series

Radar, Book 1

Legend, Book 2

About This Book

Having cultivated his instincts through years of naval missions, Radar is roaming the world, working part-time for Levi and Bullard. When he's instructed to go to Paris to help out a new start-up, he's not sure what to expect. Especially given the caginess of Levi's description of those who Radar would be working for. Outside of telling him, *He'd fit right in*, there is minimal intel on the job itself. Plus Radar's working with two men he doesn't know, and they aren't willing to share their own secrets.

Sammy threw in her heart and soul to help her best friend and fellow hacker track down a bomber, who'd left devastation behind on the Parisian streets over the last few years. When they finally get something tangible, they contact the authorities to help. That's when Sammy's world goes to hell.

The race to save Sammy—and, indeed, Paris from an imminent attack—has Radar questioning his own instincts, and the abilities of those around him. … especially Sammy's.

Sign up to be notified of all Dale's releases here!
https://geni.us/DaleNews

PROLOGUE

IT HAD BEEN weeks since the chaotic mass wedding and the biggest party that Terkel had ever attended in his life. That it was all for him and his friends and his team had filled his heart with joy and had reminded him what was important in life. Now, as he eyed his wife's protruding belly, he realized that they still had a ton more work to do—turning this old castle outside of London into their team's new headquarters. He looked over at Gage. "We need to do an assessment of what still needs to happen here in the next little bit."

"We're also getting calls for help." Gage frowned, then said, "I wasn't going to mention it Terk, but he's called twice today already."

"Who?"

"Jonas. He wants to talk to you."

"What does he want?" Terk asked.

Gage shook his head. "I've been pushing him off because I know, as soon as I call him back, our free time here will come to an end."

"It will change for sure," Terk murmured. "We can't get out of that."

"I know. I know," Gage admitted. "I was still trying though."

Terk burst into laughter, nodding. "It's been pretty special. Crazy at times, with all this work on the place and all. It seems even those who left after the weddings are back today."

"And that will change things too," Gage noted.

Even as they talked, Damon and Tasha walked in the door, all smiles and hugs.

"You guys look great," Terk said.

"You should try getting away every once in a while," Damon suggested.

"And I would, but, right now, this place is still a nightmare." Terk shrugged.

Damon raised his eyebrows, as he looked around. "It's looking phenomenal."

"We're getting there," Terk acknowledged. "We're not quite there yet, but we're close." Then he studied the newlyweds, smiled, and asked, "Are you guys ready to get back to work?"

Damon and Tasha both nodded. "Yeah, it was good to get away, but honestly we missed you guys," Tasha said, as she walked over and gave Terk a big hug. "And now, after confirming that I'm pregnant, I'm so excited. I really just want to be home with family."

Damon nodded. "Even when I told her that we could stay longer, she was like, *Nope, I want to go home*," he said, with a big smile.

"So, that's where we're at, and that's good," Terk replied, "because you really do want to know who your friends are and where you'll be in these times to come."

"Exactly," Tasha stated. "And, with that, I'm heading upstairs. I might even have a nap." She laughed, rolling her eyes, and quickly disappeared.

"She hasn't quite adjusted to the fact that she has zero energy. And it's still early in her pregnancy," Damon shared.

"So she's not sure what that means."

"It means she's pregnant," Celia declared, as she waddled into the kitchen.

Damon took one look at her and winced. "My God, I sure hope Tasha is not carrying twins."

Celia chuckled. "I have no clue what she's carrying. And, right now, it's all I can do to keep my own world somewhat contained."

Damon nodded. "I hear you there," he murmured. "So what's going on?"

Terk replied, "Jonas is being insistent this morning. He's called a couple times already." Just then, Terk checked his phone. "I had mine off," he confessed. Reluctantly he turned it back on, and it rang immediately. "Well, here we go." He frowned, switching it to Speaker. "Jonas, what's up?"

"Don't you guys ever answer your phones?" he asked in exasperation.

"Sorry, mine was off," Terk stated. "What can I do for you?"

"What you can do for us is give us some help," he snapped. "We have two escaped prisoners."

"More escaped prisoners?" Terk asked in a drawling voice.

"Hey, they were being transported from France," he clarified, "and now the shit's hit the fan."

"Who are these prisoners?"

"They're wanted by Interpol, but we wanted first crack to interrogate them, so they were being transported," he said. "However, on the way, somehow they escaped."

"Did they go via the tunnel or the ferry?"

"Yeah, we're still trying to get the details on all that," Jonas replied. "I'm sending over the information I have right now. We really need these guys, and we need them back now."

"And why are you calling us?" Terk asked.

At that question, Jonas sighed. "Because there's a problem."

"What kind of problem?"

"We weren't supposed to have them in the first place," he shared reluctantly. "So none of this can come back to us."

"Great, so we're supposed to do a catch-and-retrieve mission, and you don't want anybody to know you guys did the original catch?"

"No one can know that and no one can know that you were hired by us. So I hope you guys have your banking set up because we have the budget to pay you."

When he named the figure, everybody in the room was stunned, and they just stared at each other, their eyebrows sky-high. An audible silence took over, as they contemplated the monies involved.

"Fifty percent now, fifty percent when you bring them in," Jonas confirmed. "I can't tell you how important it is for your future possibility of working with us if you can do this. … If you can't? Well, I can't guarantee too much more work."

"Send us what you've got," Terk said, "and I'll see who I've got available."

"If you don't have anybody available because you're all still sitting around in whatever marital-bliss thing you guys have going on over there, not to mention the baby factory," he added, with a snort, "you need to hire somebody."

"Oh, I definitely need to hire several somebodies." Terk groaned. "Still I wouldn't send them out on a mission all alone," he stated, knowing that, when working previously for the US government, Terk's team had always been the intel gatherers, the secret weapon in the background, not necessarily the front-runners. "We must ensure they're good enough to even go on a job in our name."

"That's your problem," Jonas declared. "You have literally four hours to get back to me. Well, no, you *had* four, but now you only have one. You would have had longer, but you didn't answer your damn phone." And, with that, Jonas disconnected.

Terk addressed the group, "You heard the figures."

"Yeah, we sure did," Gage said, "and we definitely need the money for our own satellite, so I'm willing." He looked around at the others. "Who's coming with me?"

Calum spoke up. "And that's the problem. We normally work as a team. Two to four of us. Now it's a whole different ball game. Are we doing this alone or what?" Calum asked. "Do you think this is a two-man job or four?"

"Even if four, we can't leave this place unprotected," Terk noted. "An awful lot of very important people are here. … So we need a plan in place. However, let's not forgot that we have two other teams we can work with as well."

"Right." Calum nodded. "Levi and Bullard, correct? But, if that's the case, and we need help this time, then they must send men to London or Paris, just to be local for this job. So maybe save their men for the next job?"

Terk frowned, contemplating that logistics issue. He pulled out his phone and pressed a speed dial number. "Levi, do you have anyone close to us?"

"I know of some over there," Levi said cautiously. "Why are you asking?"

"Jonas has a job for us, but we're hardly set up with the

manpower yet."

"That is something we need to sort out. I could have someone at your place in a few days—if you're set up for team members moving in?"

"If you know anyone available today, call me. Otherwise send this guy," Terk replied abruptly. "We'll find room regardless. If we can pull off this job, I suspect we'll get very busy, very quickly."

With that he disconnected and looked around at the group. "I was contacted by someone not too long ago," he shared, checking his phone. "It's one of the reasons I had turned this off, so I could think about it. Anyway, his name is Riff, and I used to know him, and he sent out the word that he was looking for work," Terk explained. "I just wasn't sure that we were ready to hire anybody."

"Probably not, but, if we'll be taking MI6 jobs," Damon suggested, "we need more people, particularly given the pregnancies right now."

"I agree," Terk stated. "I just didn't want to start down that road so soon. I was hoping to have, say, a half-dozen men from Levi and Ice, and, if we were so lucky, the same from Bullard. But that means additional housing, cooks, weapons, etc. And we're not there yet."

"I don't think we have a choice," Damon pointed out quietly. "What's the deal with this Riff guy, the possible new hire?"

Before Terk could respond, Wade stepped forward. "I know him. ... He was always a little different."

"He's definitely a little different," Terk confirmed, "because his abilities are a little different."

"He has abilities?" Damon stared at Terk in delight. "So how come you haven't hired him before?"

"A couple reasons. Before, he couldn't pass muster with the CIA."

"Why was that?" Damon asked.

"Because he was once suspected in a murder case, and they steer clear of that messiness."

"Ouch, whose murder?" Gage asked.

"His fiancée's," Terk said.

"And did he kill her?"

"No, he didn't," Terk replied, "but it affected him badly."

"Yeah, you're not kidding," Gage stated. "Can you imagine? Not only dealing with the grief and the loss but you also have to deal with the rest of the world suspecting you."

"Exactly." Terk nodded. "I know he didn't do it, and he knows he didn't do it, but it's really a matter of whether any of you will have an issue with it."

"If you trust him, I'm willing to give Riff a try," Damon said. "Send him out with me. I'll put him through the wringer."

"One more thing," Terk added, "and it's one of the reasons Riff called me in the first place. He'll be looking for help as well."

"What kind of help?" Damon asked.

"He still hasn't found out who killed his fiancée," Terk replied. "As you can imagine, he needs to resolve that issue, before he can move on." Just then his phone buzzed. *Levi.* "That was fast," Terk said, with a smile.

"Radar is in Paris. I called him. Give the word, and he's yours. He was doing a job in Africa, then headed to France to see some family."

"We want him," Terk said immediately, walking over to a whiteboard, full of house renovations in progress. He grabbed a corner and started writing. "Give me his contact information. I'll set it up."

"And Ice will invoice you for him," Levi replied, laughing. "This will work out well for all of us."

"Ha," Terk muttered. "Says you. We need our shit here operational, and I wouldn't have said we were there yet."

"Doesn't matter. You'll learn on the fly." And, with that, Levi shared Radar's information, signing off with, "He's waiting for you."

Terk stared down at his phone, then lifted his gaze to his team. "Thoughts?"

"Radar, Riff, and me," Gage said immediately. "Damon too, if need be." Gage looked at the others. "Unless anyone has something to say about Riff?" With nobody objecting, Gage added, "Still, if we can't widen our base, we'll have to send out one to two new men on each and every job. Although, if Riff comes to work with us, he comes with conditions. We'd have to foot the bill for that."

"If Riff comes to work for us, of course we would help him solve his own matter too," Wade confirmed. "I say, give Riff a call, and let's get started. And, while you're working with Riff, maybe get the information on his fiancée's murder, so we can start researching the details and possibly get this sorted quickly, after this catch-and-retrieve is completed."

Terk nodded. "Any objections?" he asked, but there were none. "Okay then, I'll give Riff a call, and one of you call Jonas. Tell him that, if he's got that kind of money sitting around, we have no problem taking it off his hands." Then with a big fat grin, he said, "Looks like we're in business, ladies and gents."

"We still need a company name though," Wade reminded him.

"And I have one." Terk hesitated. "It's partly from this castle. Above the door in Latin, roughly translated, it says, *In times of war, … we guard.*"

The others looked at him in surprise.

"I was thinking, *Guardian Security.*"

"And for short, … because you know it'll happen"— Wade gave a fat grin—"*Terk's Guardians.*"

CHAPTER 1

RADAR—OR ROBERT DAGLIESH, a name he barely recognized anymore—studied the lanes of traffic speeding past him. He was on the Calais side of the tunnel, crossing from France to England, in the immediate vicinity where the people had disappeared. He'd walked as close as he could get to where the abandoned vehicle had been found, then towed to the side, out of the way to keep traffic flowing. Of course nothing to see onsite. However, he had to admire the choice of location for a kidnapping.

The traffic at the time had been heavy, with steadily moving vehicles. They were in broad daylight, and the kidnapping, or worse, had happened fast enough that no one understood what was going on. There'd been enough room for the vehicles behind to drive around the empty vehicle, and that had kept many from stopping to inform the authorities that something was amiss—at least amiss enough to contact law enforcement and not just port authorities.

Several of the surrounding vehicles' license plates had been caught on cameras, and the respective owners had been telephoned to see if they'd seen anything.

It wasn't a big surprise that most hadn't seen anything, other than a few people walking around a vehicle that had obviously broken down. As the traffic had been heavy, most of the drivers had been focused on getting to the next part of their journey, rather than watching what anyone else was doing.

The port itself was huge and moved with incredible efficiency, as they moved thousands of people back and forth. Any broken-down vehicle was towed out of the way and dealt with via the same efficiency. Only after several hours did anyone understand that the vehicle was more important than anyone had thought.

Of course all intel was out of Radar's reach just yet, although he'd texted Terk several times, sending the bits of information he'd gathered on the issue.

Hell, by rights, Radar shouldn't even be here. He'd just come from helping out Bullard on several jobs, when Levi had suggested that Radar travel to England to meet Terk.

"Hey, they are your kind of people," Levi had declared.

"What the hell does that mean?" Radar had asked. "Since when do I have a 'kind of people'?"

Levi's gaze never wavered, and that straight knowing look had been eerie, coming from such steady eyes. "We all have a 'kind' of people. And I guarantee that Terk is yours."

"And you aren't?"

Levi's grin flashed, even matching the flash in his gaze. "Absolutely. Terk is our kind of people too, yet in a different manner."

The way Levi had worded that bizarre exchange had made Radar back off slightly. He'd spent a lifetime being … different. And he wasn't, not as far as he could see. However, he'd always felt it. Like some *faking it until he made it* type of thing. Joining the military had changed all that, but, every once in a while, his *difference* still reared its ugly head. Like now.

Who the hell was this Terk guy anyway?

So far, wandering Calais, waiting for the rest of this hastily put together team to pick him up, Radar could only wonder what he'd gotten himself into.

JUST AS GAGE took a seat on a small local flight, he texted Terk. **Things to put on the damn list are airplane, airport, helicopter, helipad.**

He settled back and buckled in, wondering what the hell this trip would be all about. His phone buzzed, as the file from Jonas finally downloaded. Time was beyond being of the essence at this point, but, as he read Terk's incoming message, he learned that Radar was apparently already on the other side of the tunnel. He was tasked with checking the area for possibilities and looking to see if anybody could have gotten off and escaped. He was also questioning the city's ground staff, plus looking at tech options for hacking into the tunnel cameras. Terk was apparently still waiting for official permission from Jonas for that, before Terk's team hit it unofficially.

Gage just snorted and stared out the window. This would be one of those times when permission would be a given, otherwise the work would never get done and why bother hiring them. The fact that they had very little information on where these four people went missing—the two persons of interest and the two British MI6 agents who came to intercept them, but all four were then captured—was already a problem.

What happened to the French guys on this original transport assignment? Had they gone missing too? Surely France needed two men to transport two detainees. Jonas had left way too much unsaid, and that raised a whole different set of questions. Had the French transporters been bribed, knocked out, or taken out? Gage hoped it was bribed. Taken out was all too common in scenarios such as this, but one could only hope this wouldn't end up that ugly.

The flight was short, which was a good thing. Gage had just enough time to go through the little bits of information and to write up a list of questions. He fired the questions off to Terk, not knowing whether these queries should go directly to Jonas or not, but figured that maybe, for the moment, it would be better to go this way. Later, if Gage didn't get answers fast enough, he'd be on Jonas's case pretty damn quick. As far as Gage figured, he had about thirty minutes, and then he'd blow up Jonas's phone.

When Gage finally deplaned, he looked around the airport, grabbed the rental vehicle that Tasha had arranged, and headed for the tunnel—or the *chunnel,* as some called it. That would be faster and would save him some time, compared to going over on the ferry. He phoned Terk, setting the phone on his dash. "I picked up the rental, and I'm inching my way toward the entrance to the tunnel. What's the status?"

"Riff has agreed to help, and he's currently on your side of the tunnel. Radar is waiting on the other side for you."

"Sounds good. Any chance Riff has done reconnaissance yet?"

"I'll let him update you. I gave him your license plate number, so keep your passenger door unlocked, and I suspect he'll join you in a few minutes."

"Good thing you warned me. So, you've got Radar on the other side, correct? Send me a picture of him and Riff, would ya?"

Since Radar and Riff were both people he hadn't worked with before, Gage felt his own guards coming up; yet he left just enough allowance for a probe. As much as he wanted to think he was back to full strength, he couldn't help but keep some of his blocks in place, just to keep Lorelei safe back at Guardian central. He smirked at that. "Really? The *Guardians*? Isn't that a little trite?" Yet it was catchy.

He inched forward at a crawl, when the passenger door opened unexpectedly. Jolted, he turned in time to see a six-foot-four heavily muscled frame slide into the truck beside him. Gage gave the stranger a hard look—hard to miss Riff's seemingly permanent scowl or the *leave me the hell alone* vibe that radiated off him as well. Gage had to think this guy was different before, back when his fiancée was alive. Riff was a tormented soul right now. Gage turned back to face the windshield. "Hello, Riff," Gage replied calmly. "I'm Gage."

Riff gave a clipped nod, not saying anything.

"Did you get a chance to do any reconnaissance?"

Riff again nodded. "Yeah, though nothing to see. If anybody left from here, there aren't any tracks. We don't have access to the tunnel's cameras as yet."

"Yeah, we'll get Tasha and Sophia on that, depending on how Radar is doing on that subject."

At that, Riff turned to look at him. "They'll have to hack into it."

"Maybe, maybe not," Gage muttered. He quickly hit Dial on Terk's number, and, when Terk answered, Gage began, "Riff is here beside me. Nothing to see or hear at this point."

At that, Riff leaned forward to the phone. "Terk."

It seemed more of an acknowledgment than anything else.

Terk, with a smile in his tone, said, "Hey, Riff. Good to hear your voice."

"Says you," he bantered comfortably. "I don't have the means to hack into the computers here."

"No, we're giving MI6 another ten minutes to give us permission. After that, we'll do it on our own. Radar is hacking France's side, while we work on access from our side."

At that, Riff looked over at Gage but leaned forward slightly to speak to the phone. "Terk, do you have what's needed to do the hacking? I don't mean the run-of-the-mill stuff but top secret black-level access."

"Yep," Terk replied, his tone complacent.

Gage gave Riff a feral grin. "Facilities and personnel both."

Riff's eyebrows shot up, and then he gave an approving nod. "Good thing. I'm hoping for a fast job myself."

"Were you able to get a line on what happened to your fiancée?" Gage asked.

Riff's shoulders stiffened, and he settled back against the passenger seat. "I got a name."

"Give me the name," Terk said, but Riff hesitated. "Come on, Riff. We can do all the background runs and pull information you may not have accessed yet," Terk added. "That'll take some time. So, while you're doing this MI6 op, we can help you out with that."

"His name's Argyle, Argyle McNamara."

"Okay, and we'll need some information about where she was killed, what she was doing, and that sort of thing. Just give me anything you can think of, relevant or not."

"I already emailed you the file," Riff muttered solemnly. "You've got from now to when we wrap up this job to get as much information as you can."

"Then what?" Gage asked, pulling the truck forward as he followed the line of traffic.

"Then I'm off on my own."

Terk interrupted, "I'll stay on the line in the background for a while, so I can update you as developments occur."

"Some of these jobs are easier to do when you've got backup," Gage suggested to Riff, trying to keep his tone mild. He sensed the anger and frustration radiating off the man at his side. However, the strong wall surrounding the man interested Gage the most. They hadn't had a chance to even ask Terk about what Riff's abilities were, and, from just looking at him, it wasn't anything Gage could see. Yet the man had a shield like Gage had never seen before. He sent Terk a communique telepathically. *What are Riff's abilities?*

The response came back a little garbled. *They're changing on him. So control is an issue. He's so full of anger and frustration that I'm worried about what happens afterward.*

Great, so you sent me out with somebody who's a ticking bomb? Gage snorted. *Like I need that shit.*

Oh, I don't think he is a danger to you or to any of us, Terk clarified. *Still, when he finds whoever killed his fiancée …*

Got it. Gage gave a slight headshake, as he stared out at traffic, moving his vehicle through the tunnel. It tested his patience to just sit idle for so long, waiting to get through.

"Do we have any intel on the kidnapping?" Riff asked Terk. "Hard to act without it."

Terk replied, "I'll send you the file. We don't have much." While Riff waited for the download, Terk gave him the rundown. "Apparently MI6 did a silent catch-and-retrieve, but somehow lost track of both their two persons of interest and two of their own guys, somewhere between here and there."

"This isn't exactly an easy place to kidnap anybody," Riff noted.

"No, it's not," Terk agreed. "I suspect that they lost them on the other side, and either were given decoys or were taken out before they got very far. Gotta run." Then Terk disconnected.

"The intel is sparse," Riff noted.

"Yeah, one of those secret under-the-radar missions, and, on top of that, everybody disappeared."

"So, what? … Just *poof*?" Riff snapped. "And nobody knows what the hell happened? No getaway vehicle? No bodies? Ours or theirs?"

"Exactly. No one. All MI6 had was confirmation of the catch."

Riff didn't say anything, but he settled back and studied his phone, as the information came in. He shook his head. "Is MI6 still as useless as ever?"

Gage cracked a smile. "I'm pretty sure they would hate to hear my answer, but, in many ways, I would say yes. We have one person there we work with exclusively."

Riff snorted. "Don't tell me. … Jonas."

At that, Gage glanced at the newcomer and then slowly nodded. "Yes, Jonas."

Riff gave a one-arm shrug. "At least Jonas is a square shooter. I dealt with him once or twice, and he was okay."

"What did you do before this?"

"I worked for a private security firm … in France."

At that, Gage stiffened and glared at him. "Did you have anything to do with that mess with Bullard?"

"No, I had moved on before Bullard came in and blew up everything. It was for the better though. Things were getting pretty ugly. There's quite a bit more work to be done to straighten things up over there."

"I hear you." Gage swore, as he thought about it. "We had a hell of a time getting Bullard back home."

"The fact that you even found him and got him back again is pretty amazing. Not to mention that most of the core team survived it all. Those guys don't fool around."

"None of us do," Gage declared.

Riff turned and glared at him, his eyes blazing an almost golden color. "Look. I've known Terk for years," Riff stated, "and we've known *of* each other for far longer than that, but I don't know you at all."

Gage felt something roiling inside Riff, teeming with anger, and Gage nodded. "You will after this."

RIFF STUDIED THE man called Gage at his side, noting his calm competence and balanced energy. It made Riff feel somewhat better. Terk had always been a bit of a wild card, so Riff knew to be prepared and to expect the unexpected because, with Terk, you never really knew what he was up to or who he was up to it with. Riff knew that, despite Terk going private, he still probably had government contacts and ties to the CIA, and that in itself was enough to keep Riff wary. "According to Terk, things have been tough for you guys."

"You think? Just like Bullard, we were attacked. Only, in our case, we were attacked from within."

"What did you expect?" Riff snorted in disgust. "You were working for the government. And, when they close down a program, ... they permanently close down the program."

"Yeah, you got any firsthand experience of that?"

Riff snorted. "Yep, I sure do, and I haven't worked for the government since."

"You okay to have MI6 foot this bill?"

"Money is money," he stated succinctly, "but only on a contract basis. Now I am okay because my contract is with Terk, and money doesn't come into it."

Gage smiled at that. "Yep. He told us."

"He didn't tell you much because I don't know much. Bottom line for me is solving this op and fast. So I can get back to my case."

Just then Gage's phone rang. He answered it. However, the static was so awful that he quickly sent Terk a message. *A phone call is coming in, but service is too bad out here, until we're on the other side.* Then he provided the number.

With that, Terk soon responded. *It's Radar. I'll talk to him.*

Gage sat back and waited. They had another twenty minutes or so to go in the tunnel. By the time Terk got back to Gage, it had been almost that long. "What took you so long?" Gage snapped into the phone, then realized he'd said it out loud because Riff was staring at him, that golden gaze blazing, as he hadn't heard the earlier telepathic part of the conversation.

Well, that was one skill Riff didn't have. *Yet.*

Terk replied, "Radar found somebody who saw two men open up a lorry and pull two people out and put them in another vehicle. We've got license plates on both. The one lorry ended up snarling up traffic, heading toward the tunnel from that side for quite a while. However, it was found empty, keys in the ignition, but nobody in the vehicle. The service had to come in and remove it, which backed up traffic."

"Yet the witness only saw two people remove the two occupants from the back?"

"So it could have been the driver and passenger get out, walk around to the back, open it up and remove the persons of interest and walk away?" Gage looked over at Riff, who was listening intently.

"It's possible," Terk replied, his voice trailing off a bit. "Radar doesn't have much of a description on any of the four because the witness wasn't close enough. The witness did say that he didn't see anybody inside the lorry get out before these two approached the back of the truck. So maybe the two transport people were already gone. We're looking into the camera feed, and, since we've had no response from Jonas, we hacked into the transit system, looking for clues."

"Good enough. And the vehicles?" Gage asked.

"The lorry we already know is empty and has been towed by the French police. So, our one piece of evidence is sitting in their impound yard. Again we've requested access via MI6 to hack into the DGSE. No answer as of yet, so have no idea whether the towed vehicle is helpful."

"Any info on the car the kidnap victims were put into?"

"It was found on the side of the road off one of the main highways, not twenty minutes from the ferry terminals."

"Of course. So they were moved into a third vehicle."

"Exactly," Terk confirmed. "What we don't have is cameras with eyes on that car."

"Dammit," Gage snapped, only to lean forward, studying their surroundings. "Okay, we're almost out."

"When you exit the tunnel, watch for the first large mileage sign to Paris and pull off to the side. Radar will join you there."

"Good enough."

And, sure enough, standing at the designated sign was another dangerous-looking man—with an offsetting pair of dimples on his cheeks—dressed all in black, his arms crossed over his chest, as he leaned nonchalantly against the sign post. Gage pulled up, and the stranger hopped in. Just as fast as that, Gage swerved back out into the traffic.

"So, where are we going?" Riff asked, ignoring the new arrival.

"Hi, Radar. How are you doing?" Radar said in a mocking tone. "Apparently you're Gage and Riff."

"Yeah, that's right," Gage replied, "and you were working for Bullard?"

"Bullard and Levi actually. I was over helping out Bullard, then took a few days to see family around here, before I headed back to Africa. Levi asked me to step in and to give you guys a hand, since I was here already. You're a new outfit, *huh*?" he asked Gage, with a note of concern in his voice. "A startup, so to speak?"

Gage gave a shout of laughter. "The company itself might be new, but believe me. We're old hands at this."

"If you say so."

"I say so. Things might be off to a rocky start in some ways in terms of paperwork and the like, but we know the job."

"Good," Radar replied. "According to the one eyewitness account, the two persons of interest were taken to a small car, which has now been located on the London side of the channel."

"Did you have any descriptions of the two people who were moved?" Gage asked.

"One tall, one slight," Radar noted. "That's all we got. Both dressed in black, both with long hair. Nothing else. … Do you not even know who these people are?" Radar asked suddenly.

"I do have their names on file," Gage replied, "and the team is doing a workup, as we speak."

"Should have had a full workup before we ever got this far," Riff snorted in disgust.

"Sure," Gage agreed, "but considering that we were first contacted about this only three hours ago, I think we're doing fine."

"You do also know that three hours is three hours too many, right?" Radar murmured.

"Of course I do," Gage shot back, "and, right now, I'm looking for any connection to give us a direction to go."

"Great," Radar mumbled, as he settled back. "So, this is really just a joy ride."

CHAPTER 2

RADAR WASN'T EVEN sure what he was doing here. Levi had said that these guys needed somebody to help out, so had volunteered Radar. It likely had something to do with Levi believing that Terk was Radar's kind of people. Again that had Radar wondering just what the hell that meant. He wasn't sure what *normal* meant. Yet, at the same time, he was more than willing to make it seem he could do the job. And he could do that without reservation.

Maybe he read the whole thing wrong, but he'd taken Levi's comment to mean that the others were not normal somehow. And something *was* odd about both of these guys in the car that Radar hadn't yet put his finger on—though, in fairness, the guy in the front passenger seat hadn't spoken after the first couple replies.

Radar pulled out his phone and quickly texted Levi. **Connected. Really don't have a clue where we're going from here.**

Levi sent him a thumbs-up and a message. **Patience. They do know what they're doing.**

Radar wasn't so sure about that, but, hey, having worked for both Levi and Bullard, plus many private jobs over the last ten years, Radar was willing to sit back and take an easy one. The fact that three were on the team was already good odds.

One of the phones up on the dash rang. Gage hit the Speaker button, then said, "Hey, Terk, all three here."

"Good." Then he read off a street address. "Head there."

At that, Radar leaned forward watching as Gage punched it into a GPS. "What's there?"

"It's the address where the two persons of interest were taken from," Gage shared.

"Do we have any idea why they were taken?"

"Apparently they had intel on a bombing that MI6 was looking to prevent. Those two were the ones with the information."

"On the bombing or the bomb maker?" Riff asked, his voice quiet. "We've had quite a problem in Europe with somebody making a very specialized bomb. We've had malls in Czechoslovakia, Germany, and Switzerland blasted in the last six months."

"That's the one," Terk confirmed, his voice hard. "Both of these people apparently have had some contact with him. They were being moved to MI6 for further debriefing."

"With MI6 employees?"

"Not according to Jonas, but he's been pretty cagey about that."

"Of course he has," Riff stated, disgruntled. "He's government."

At that, Radar laughed. "Isn't that the truth," he muttered. "Hey, Terk, can you give us a full workup on these two persons of interest?"

"Should hit your phone in about five seconds," Terk said and disconnected the call, just as all their phones buzzed.

Radar stared down at his phone and asked, "So, was that a lucky guess on the timing?" Neither of the men in the front answered. Radar sat back and frowned. "Okay, so what the hell's going on here?" he muttered, ignoring the eerie sensation in the back of his mind, as he brought up his phone and checked out the information. "I didn't realize one was a woman," he noted, frowning.

"Does it matter?" Riff asked.

"No, not really," Radar admitted. "I just hate to see women in these situations."

"Got it," Gage replied. "Particularly if they're helpless, right?"

"Aren't all women helpless?" Radar quipped, and then he laughed. "Scratch that. If anybody called Ice helpless, they'd get their butt kicked across the room."

Gage nodded. "Not to mention that a lot of her team would say the same thing these days. Plus, if you ever said that to the partners of my team, I can't even imagine what their response would be."

Radar looked over at him. "How many on your team?"

"Eight and counting. Plus eight particularly skilled partners."

At that, Riff turned and eyed Gage. "Terk really found a partner, *huh?*"

Gage didn't say anything, but he gave a clipped nod. "In a way that you would never quite believe."

"And you won't tell us either, I suppose," Radar asked jokingly. "What a pain in the ass it is to only get bits and pieces of stories."

"It depends on where you end up working after this," Gage declared, "but an awful lot of stuff at my place you may or may not end up liking."

"I've always heard some weird things about your team. Yet nobody really talks about it."

"Nope, and *weird* is a good way to put it."

"I don't do weird," Radar stated. Then he winced because many considered him beyond weird. However, few knew *how* weird, and he definitely didn't volunteer that info to people he didn't know.

"That's fine," Gage said. "I understand, and you don't have to if you don't want to. We're just looking for somebody who can function with our team and who can do the work that we need. That is all that matters."

"That's your problem then." Radar turned and glared at Riff. "What do you do? Same weird shit?"

"I don't give a shit if anybody thinks it's weird or not," Riff snapped, his tone gravelly. "I do the work."

"Right. Good point." Frowning at that, Radar settled back and studied the files. "I could use more information on her."

"What information do you want? Send the request to Terk or Levi," Gage suggested. "Levi's satellites are up. Ours are not. So better him maybe."

"Bullard has satellites up too. How come you guys don't?"

"It's in the works," Gage shared. "As I mentioned earlier, we're still getting a lot of things set up."

Radar shrugged at that. "That's bound to take some time. Setting up a satellite is not exactly something you order on a Monday and get installed on a Tuesday."

Gage laughed. "No, it sure isn't. It will probably be at least six months."

"Good thing you're friends with Levi and Bullard then."

"More than friends, we're all family of sorts," Gage stated. "It's just, on our side, it's more like the Addams family."

That startled a choke of laughter out of Riff, who had been largely silent.

"*Okay,*" Radar said, still studying the two men. They looked normal and on the up-and-up, except they had that hard edge of people who had seen too much in life. Radar had seen that before in other men, in other team members. Radar hadn't seen quite as much as they had.

Something was also very guarded about them. Radar wasn't so sure he liked that, but it wasn't exactly something he could change. They were who they were, and Radar would just get along, do the job, then figure out what he wanted to do after this. Levi had given him a little info on Terk but not enough to assay the mystery. Radar knew nothing of Riff at all.

"I'll read the file later," Gage stated, keeping his eyes on the road, "so give me a rundown."

"The female, Savannah—but for some reason is known as Sammy to people close to her—is twenty-nine and a computer programmer."

"Now that's interesting," Gage noted. "What would she know about the bombing?"

Riff replied without hesitation, "She's been tracking the bomb maker."

Both Gage and Radar shot Riff a frown. "How do you know that?" Gage asked.

"A little birdie told me," Riff said succinctly.

Gaged nodded, as if it were totally normal.

But, for Radar in the backseat, it just added to his mounting unease. He sent Levi a text. **All right, what's going on with these two? How do they know things that aren't in the files?**

Levi sent back a reminder. **They've been doing this for a long time. They have an awful lot of networking sources that you don't have yet.**

That made good sense, so Radar settled back, prepared to give them a little more space. "I also think we should go to her residence," he finally suggested.

"Why is that?" Gage asked.

"Just thinking that she's probably got a boyfriend or a partner or maybe a roommate. So, chances are, someone would know what she was up to, where she got the information from, and who might have been after her. It's worth a shot anyway."

"Good point," Gage stated. Then he glanced at Riff. "You want to check with Jonas and see if anybody has done that?"

Riff's face split into a grin for the first time, and he chuckled. Gage looked at him and laughed out loud.

"What am I missing?" Radar asked.

"You're not missing anything," Gage replied, "except that Riff hates the guy. So, asking him to phone MI6 was a bit out there. Sorry, I was just being a smart-ass."

"Oh, I'm more than happy to call him," Riff declared. "I've been looking for a chance to give them shit."

"Well, maybe not too much shit," Gage suggested. "We need information, and we need it fast, and, if there is anything on the female computer programmer, that information must be in her MI6 files. We need it, and Jonas is our only connection at the moment."

"Will do." At that, Riff picked up his phone, started dialing, and quickly put in the request.

Radar just shook his head. In the back seat and clearly out of the loop, it was hard to get information from a one-sided conversation. He went back to reading the file and quickly checked the intel on the other person who had gone missing with Sammy—some guy she worked with who had a wife and two little kids. The guy was basically geek material. Caught hacking as a teenager, he'd gone straight, was hired by the government, and has been working with them ever since. "The second guy doesn't send up any flags. The fact that the first file, the one on Sammy, is incomplete does though."

"I hear you," Gage replied.

Radar looked up to see Gage studying him in the rearview mirror, a smirk on his face. "Problems?" Radar challenged.

Gage shook his head. "No, none." Once the GPS started talking to him, he quickly shifted lanes. Following directions, he pulled into an address.

Radar realized for the first time just how quickly the trip had gone by. He stopped and looked up at the building on their side of the street. Then he studied the rest of the file, looking for any information. When his phone buzzed, it was more information coming in. He was loving the communication system, and it moved smoothly enough, just like Levi's and Bullard's jobs. These guys may have been new to him, but they were obviously total pros. Or at least held up a good front. "According to the latest download, there's no boyfriend, but she has a restraining order against an ex-boyfriend," Radar shared. "I like him for this."

Riff in the front seat snorted. "Doesn't mean anything if you do. We got no evidence pointing to him."

"No, but now we're at her Paris apartment." Radar hopped out, pocketed his phone, and searched the area in a quick sweep. He caught Gage doing something too—just standing there, looking too focused on something that was not there, or at least it wasn't in front of him. Radar asked Gage, "What the hell are you doing?"

Gage quirked his lips and said, "I'm checking out the area."

"Yeah, well, I can do that too," Radar replied, with an eye roll.

Riff just stared at him. "He has skills you have no idea about." Riff's dark tone sounded like a threat. "I suggest you knock off the laughter." And, with that, he turned and marched up the front steps and opened the front door to the building. Gage followed along behind at a slower pace.

Radar looked around, studied the area, and swore. "This is completely open to anybody. There's no security and the neighborhood? … It's not even upper middle class. If they lived and worked here, chances are they were both hackers." As he walked in behind the two guys, he found then both standing at the elevator, waiting.

Radar looked at Gage and said, "I'll take the stairs." Heading to the stairwell, he raced up the three flights and met nobody on the way up. As he headed down the hallway to the apartment they were looking for, he heard noises somewhere ahead. As he got to the door of the apartment that they needed, the elevators opened, and Gage and Riff raced out.

Radar frowned at them and motioned at the open door. Pulling out his weapon, he kicked the door fully open with his foot and marched in. There he caught sight of two men tossing the place.

Both turned, hands in the air. "Whoa, whoa, whoa," one called out.

Radar gave the first guy a half smile. "So nice to know this is how you treat a lady's place. She's your ex, right? No wonder she's got a restraining order against you."

The guy flushed. "What the hell do you know about

this, man? Sammy is supposed to be here, and she's not. Something has happened to her."

"Yeah? So, you came and what? Destroyed her place to make it look like some B&E?"

"You got her body stashed somewhere?" Gage asked the stranger from behind Radar.

But the man just flushed brighter, then shook his head. "No way, man. But she owes me money."

At that, Radar motioned to the floor. "Face down, hands on the ground."

"Hey, we didn't do anything wrong."

"You're destroying her property, and that's good enough for me. Now get your ass down there."

With both men on the floor, Radar turned to find Gage at the ready with zip ties. Then they quickly secured their hands. Riff effortlessly picked up the nearest guy by the back of the collar and plunked him down in the one single chair still standing. "So, tell me. What are you doing here?"

The guy looked at his buddy and wailed, "I came with him."

"Shut the fuck up," the man on the floor growled, still rolling around, glaring at his friend. "Don't say anything."

"Hey, dude. The whole game changed when we got accosted by men with guns," he declared, glaring at his friend. "You told me, 'Come on. Let's go see if there's anything to steal. … It'll be fun.' Fun, my ass. Listen. I got a buddy who works at a local pawn shop, and I could use a few bucks for some drugs. That's all this was."

He turned and glared at Riff, then Gage, before returning to Radar. "Nothing else. I don't know anything about what happened to her, and I sure as hell didn't know there was a restraining order against Pierre."

Pierre just shut his eyes and groaned. "It doesn't matter whether there is or not. She hasn't been home, and she won't be."

"Do you know Johnny?" Radar asked.

At that, Pierre's eyes popped open, and he nodded. "Yeah, her best friend, right? If he wasn't married, I'd say there was something between them. Why?"

"We're looking for Sammy." Radar stayed with the two burglars, while both Riff and Gage took a quick walk through the place. "Any idea where she's gone?"

"I told you, she's *gone*, gone."

"Yeah, and how do you know that?"

He hesitated and then shrugged. "I'm not supposed to be near her, but I came to try to talk to her and saw two guys leading them out of the apartment building into a white lorry van. They had their hands tied up."

"Did you recognize them?"

"Yeah, it was Sammy and Johnny. I just told you that."

Radar reached out and kicked him. "That's not what I meant, and you know it."

"No, man. Jesus, stop it. I didn't recognize the other two," he snapped, holding his knee close to his other one and glaring at him. "You don't have to kick me. I don't know anything."

"But this girlfriend, who you supposedly really care about, was kidnapped, and you didn't notify the police? Instead you come back here with your buddy to strip her apartment?"

At that, the buddy stared at Pierre in disgust. "Man, didn't you call the cops?"

"No, I figured somebody else would do it. She would have been protected, since she was working on some secret project."

"What secret project?" Radar asked.

"I don't know. I guess … I don't know," he cried out, twisting to look up at him. "All I know is that some people asked them to do a job on the side. I heard about it when she didn't know I was there."

"Did she have any secret hiding spots? Anything like that?" Radar asked, not sure if he believed this guy.

The guy glanced at Radar and shook his head.

Almost immediately Gage rejoined them, stepped forward, placed a hand on Pierre's forehead, and, within seconds, he stepped back. He looked at him shrewdly. "Aren't you just a little piece of shit." Without a single word, he stepped out of the room once more.

At that bizarre move, Radar looked over at Riff, but Riff was following Gage down to the bedroom. "I gather you lied," Radar pointed out.

The young guy in front of him flushed. "I hadn't had a chance to get there yet," he cried out. "If anything is in there, it's mine."

"How do you figure that? As far as I'm concerned, everything in this apartment is hers, and you are nothing but an asshole. You beat her up the last time. You remember that, right?" Radar asked, turning to look at his friend, who was horror-struck. "I guess you kept that little bit to yourself, *huh*, Pierre?"

His friend stared at Pierre on the ground. "You beat up Sammy? Jesus, she's the sweetest thing, and she would never hurt a damn fly."

"Yeah? Well, she wouldn't let me back in her life," Pierre snapped, a bit more aggro than he should have been, considering he was tied up and facing guns.

The friend shook his head, looking disgusted. "Man, what the hell happened to you? You never used to be such a piece of shit."

"Shut the fuck up," Pierre wailed, and he dropped his head onto the floor. "Godammit."

"What about the secret hiding spot of hers? What do you know about it?" Radar asked.

"I was hoping there might be something in there, and I could find out what she was up to."

"What would you do with it?" his friend asked. "If you didn't call the police when you knew she was in trouble, no way you'd call the police if you found something in her hidey-hole."

At that, Radar looked at Pierre and laughed. "You were thinking of blackmail, weren't you?"

Pierre flushed, and that was enough of a thread for Radar to pull on. "If you were thinking blackmail, you must have had some idea of how you could contact the kidnappers."

At that, Pierre's gaze shifted to the ceiling.

"You recognized one of them, didn't you?" Radar asked.

He flushed again and shook his head wildly. "No, I didn't. I really didn't."

Radar turned to find Gage walking down the hallway toward him.

Gage announced, "Pretty sure our boy here recognized one of the kidnappers and was hoping to find some blackmail material in her secret lair." Gage held up a USB key. "We've got this, but we'll need one of the laptops from the truck to figure out what it is. Who else needs to make these guys pay for what they did?"

"No way," the second young man cried out. "Man, I

didn't know what Pierre was up to. I swear. He just promised me some quick things to pawn. That's all."

"Yeah, and what would you take? If you were taking stuff, ... why would you have tossed the place?" Radar pressed on.

The buddy sat here, staring at Pierre. "Pierre said it would be fun," he muttered, as he looked around, then realized he'd been played. "But you're right. It doesn't make any sense, does it? He told me the TV was too big for me to haul out of here, and there's no sound equipment. She obviously wasn't into music, and the last thing I need is to try and sell a stupid coffeemaker." He turned and eye-murdered his buddy. "You said she had valuable items here. What the hell were you talking about?"

But Pierre was done talking, his eyes closed, as if trying to get away or at least to forget that he was tied up here.

"I imagine it's this." Gage held up the USB again.

When the door closed behind him, Radar realized Riff had gone down to the truck to get the laptop. "We'll need to make Pierre talk because he's got some idea that he could blackmail people with whatever she had stashed."

"If he could blackmail people"—Gage walked closer, studying Pierre as he lay on the ground—"that would mean that he had some way to contact them."

"Exactly. That's what I said." Radar was searching the room now. Gage looked over at Radar, then nudged his chin to the second man.

Radar stood up, then walked over to the friend, and said, "Sorry about this, bud." He then gave him a hard right uppercut to the jaw. The guy's head slipped to the side, knocked out cold. He looked over at Gage, his hands on his hips, and asked, "You want to tell me why you needed that?"

"Yeah, because nobody gets to see the shit," Gage replied. Then he bent down beside Pierre. "Pierre, I want you to talk to me."

"Fuck off," Pierre replied. "I ain't talking to you at all."

At that, Radar hit him in the same knee he had kicked before. He screamed and cried out, "Oh, you just have to torture me now, don't you?"

"I don't have to. I just need you to think about that name," Gage clarified. "And tell me how you'll contact this guy."

"I wasn't. I wasn't. I swear. I didn't know anything about it."

At that, Gage slowly straightened up, then looked over at Radar and smiled. "The guy's name was Lafontaine. ... Ah, nickname Frenchman, and they call him Frenchie because of it."

"Frenchie?" Radar's eyebrows popped up. "I know that name. Jobs were out long ago to bring him in. I heard somebody had caught him but ended up making some deal."

"Not a surprise," Gage replied. "Deals are the currency for a lot of agencies around the world. I don't know whether it involves them now or not, but, right now, it appears that Frenchie has kidnapped Sammy and Johnny. Do you know where they went and what they were after?" Gage asked Pierre.

At that, Pierre was blubbering. "I didn't tell you. I didn't tell you. How did ... If they find out, ... I didn't tell!"

"Don't worry about it," Gage said, with a wave of his hand. "You didn't tell me nothing." At that, he straightened, took a step back, and added, "We need to call the French police and tell them we found a robbery going on here."

"Yeah, that would be good." Radar stepped away. "You

do that. I'll head down to the vehicle and see what Riff has got."

"Got it," Gage confirmed, as he pulled out his phone.

At the doorway, Radar stopped and eyed Gage. "Do you have somebody to call?"

Gage quirked his lips. "Yeah, I've got somebody to call."

"Good enough." Radar closed the door behind him and bolted downstairs, but inside he was shaking. What the hell just happened, and how the hell did Gage get that name from the guy? Radar knew one person who could help him get the answers, and that's where he was headed. He hopped into the truck beside Riff and demanded, "What the bloody fucking hell was that?"

"What the hell was what?" Riff asked calmly.

"How did Gage get that name from Pierre?"

"I wasn't there, so I don't know." Riff lifted his gaze and stared at Radar. "There are plenty of methods for getting information, but I have no idea what you are referring to specifically."

"Just tell me what, … how."

Riff hesitated and then continued. "There was this group of psychics who worked for the CIA."

Radar frowned at him. "And? Was Gage one of them?" Now that notched some of Levi's innuendos, but Radar hadn't believed Levi. Yet Radar should have.

Riff shrugged. "You're welcome to ask him, if you want, but he doesn't feel very good about the CIA these days. So, if you get punched in the face, it's on you."

"So, he did work for them at one time?"

"Sure, the whole team did. Still, nobody likes those kinds of questions."

There had been talk, murmurs about Terk. "Shit, if he

can read the guy's mind—"

"Only to a certain extent, and, even then, we can't always count on the information because sometimes these guys are fed the wrong information on purpose."

"Because the right hand can't know what the left hand is doing," Radar muttered. "Wait. What? … You said *we*?"

"Exactly. Yeah, *we*. So, what we have is something very interesting on this USB. We have a location, but what we don't have is any reason why."

"But Frenchie was always involved with terrorists," Radar noted. "Do you need more than that?"

SAMMY OPENED HER eyes slowly, hoping, but nothing had changed. It was still a dimly lit room, and Johnny was still curled up, snoozing beside her on the floor. His jacket was pulled tightly around him, just like she had pulled her own hoodie tight. Why had this happened? What did they want with them? It was ridiculous.

She and Johnny had been working on this project for at least nine months without any worry of being caught. Then, all of a sudden, from one day to the next, this happened. She recognized the one young man involved in her kidnapping, as someone she had seen in passing before, yet not sure where, but she did not recognize the second one.

She knew it was confused in her mind, but, as far as she could make out, they'd been taken initially from her Paris apartment—where she and Johnny worked—by two young street punks. However, seemingly British agents intercepted them somewhere, taking her and Johnny out of the kidnappers' lorry. Then she and Johnny had been recaptured again, returning to them to Paris. She was starting to feel like a mouse in a game of catch between a dog and cat, and it was enough to drive her nuts.

Johnny reached out a hand and gently patted her knee. "It'll be okay."

"Will it?" she murmured. "Who'll grab us next?"

"Whoever it is, let's hope that they're good enough to get us away from this and to put a stop to it."

"Yeah, you're not kidding," she muttered. "I thought for sure we were rescued the first time, but do we even know what happened to those British agents?"

"No, but I don't imagine it was anything good," Johnny noted. "We were working in France to stay in the shadows, until we finished the job. I never once thought we were in danger though."

"Right, these guys are playing for keeps, aren't they?"

"Did you leave a copy behind?"

"Yeah, but it's hidden, and nobody knows where it is."

"I did too," Johnny muttered. "I just want to keep my wife and children safe."

"I don't even have anybody to worry about," she admitted. "That was one of the deciding factors to do this. I didn't have anybody who would get hurt."

He nodded. "I did it because I didn't want this bomb maker to come to Paris anymore, not after my uncle was killed."

"You're a good man," Sammy replied softly, her voice wafting in the darkness. "Besides, all we were doing was tracking his whereabouts. In a unique way, sure, but it's not as if we were hurting him."

"I know, but somebody either wants him bad or doesn't want us to know where he is."

"Or maybe both," she murmured.

Just then the door opened, and she stiffened. The light shone through the open doorway, enough that it took her eyes a few moments to adjust. Trays of food and bottles of water were brought in.

"You've got five minutes to go to the bathroom," the man stated.

She scrambled to her feet and was led outside. Johnny was taken in a separate direction. In the bathroom, she quickly washed her face, used the facilities, and then washed her hands and straightened up her hair. She took as long as she could to try to figure out if there was any way to leave a message, but preventing that was probably why these guys kept the bathroom door slightly ajar. She looked out, and her guard glared at her.

"Come on. Stop wasting my time."

He glanced around to make sure she hadn't done anything and then pushed her back into their room. Johnny was led back in behind her. She waited until he joined her on the floor, and, when he was sitting down, she looked up at the guard. "How long will you keep us here?"

He shrugged. "Until you tell us what we need to know." And, with that, he slammed the door.

She looked over at Johnny. "They took you somewhere first. Any idea why?"

"I saw them bringing in a couple other people, and one I recognized as our British guards. They're still alive, but they were tied up, blindfolded, and gagged."

She winced. "Great, so they're here too then?"

"Yeah, they're here."

She nodded. "It's weird that nobody has even asked what we know yet. He says they're keeping us until we tell them what they want to know, yet they aren't asking us any questions."

Johnny pointed, as he looked down at the food in front of him. "They gave us food at least."

She hesitated to eat, even knowing it was important to keep up her strength. It was a simple sandwich, an apple, and a bottle of water. She dove for the water first, thankful that it was sealed, so she didn't have to worry about it being poisoned or drugged. As she watched Johnny bite the sandwich with gusto, she smiled and shook her head. "Nothing could dim your appetite."

"The only thing that'll upset me is if anything threatens my family," he stated calmly.

She nodded and proceeded to eat as well. She didn't have the same drive nor the same need behind what she was doing. She wanted to help, but, in Johnny's case, he had watched his uncle get blown up in the mall on one of the main streets, and it had left an indelible mark. Johnny's wife had been pregnant with their second child at the time, and Johnny had sworn that he would do everything he could to stop this madman. This was personal for him.

The trouble was, he was a little short on information, which is why Johnny brought in Sammy on this special project. After all these months of cyberhunting, they had tracked all of Frenchie's bombings, found a headquarters— or at least they thought they did—and then realized that this madman was on the move again, from France to England. So Johnny and Sammy had reached out to both the Paris and British governments for help. Although somehow the message had become garbled after their initial attempt with Paris and getting nowhere, they'd ended up on Interpol's list. They'd reached out to the British government soon after.

Almost immediately they'd been kidnapped in France, only to have the British snag them away, and then these bad guys had taken them back again.

So, they were, indeed, in a chase, and the winning team got to keep the bomb maker.

CHAPTER 3

W HEN THE DOOR opened the second time, a different man walked in.

Sammy kept her eyes closed initially.

He spoke English, with a heavy French accent. "You have tracked Frenchie, *huh*?"

She looked up at him, trying to hide her surprise. "I don't have a name for him, but, if you're asking if it's the bomb maker, yes."

He nodded. "Lots of people go by the name Frenchie. It's just a slang term."

She nodded. "Why do you care?" she asked.

"Because we want to keep him safe."

Beside her, Johnny stiffened. She reached out a hand in the shadows and squeezed his. "I see," she replied. "So, that makes you the third then."

"How so?"

"You're the third group to kidnap us."

"Technically we were the first," he clarified, with a smile. "Because the people who brought you here were the ones who grabbed you out of your apartment. Then, of course, they lost you to the British agents." He gave her a droll look. "Believe me. They won't make that mistake again."

She nodded slowly. "And you brought us back to Paris?"

"Yep, we sure did," he confirmed cheerfully. "And here

is where you'll stay, until we can go through your materials and see what else you might know. We want to know who else you might have contacted."

Johnny spoke up. "We didn't contact anybody."

"You contacted someone in the French government," the man in front of him yelled harshly. "We want to know who and what you told them."

"We didn't know what to do with the information."

The other man nodded thoughtfully. "Who are you supposed to contact, if you're not affiliated with any groups? That makes sense." With that, he turned and walked back out, without saying any more, leaving both kidnap victims in the dark.

She whispered in a low tone, "They're affiliated with Frenchie himself. Oh my God. Now what will we do?"

"We always knew that was possible," Johnny murmured.

She groaned and laid her head back. "But that makes no sense. Nothing we have is of any interest to them. He already knows where the bomb maker's already been."

"They're probably wondering if we have some system or anything that compromises their operations. They can't have people know where Frenchie's going next."

It was a reasonable explanation. Still, it didn't make her feel better. "Ah," she muttered.

Then he lowered his voice even more and whispered, "Keep in mind, there might be audio or video surveillance in here."

"You think they've bugged this room?" she asked, squinting around the room. The dim light made it difficult to see into the corners.

"It's what I would do. And you know any of the government organizations would have. So why not these guys?"

"True, but it still sucks."

"Yep, it still sucks." He looked over at her and smiled. "See? You should have gone out more, dated more. You should have lived a little more. You never know when shit will happen."

"Yeah, but then again …" she muttered, "just remember what great choices I didn't make."

He chuckled. "You just haven't been loved."

"Is that what it is? I thought I was."

"Nope, and nope. No one can treat you like that and call it love," Johnny corrected. "You wanted to be in love, but you haven't met the right person yet."

"When I meet him, then what?"

"Then you fall in love," Johnny declared cheerfully.

"How can you be so happy right now?" she muttered, trying not to dissect his laissez-faire attitude. Why wasn't he worried? She was terrified.

He shrugged. "It's called being realistic. My wife and kids are safe, and, as long as these guys leave them alone, it's all good. We'll cooperate as much as we can and hope for survival."

She sagged back, wondering if it really were that simple. She didn't see how Johnny could possibly look at it in such a black-and-white way, but, if that worked for him, well, good. For her, it didn't seem that easy.

He patted her hand. "Listen. I've been in worse spots," he shared.

She nodded but didn't understand.

"Besides," he whispered, his tone even lower, "I think we may have a rescue coming."

At that, she stiffened her gaze, instinctively searching the small dark room. "How can you be so sure?"

"Just think about it. Two British agents have gone missing. … That is really good news for us."

"Right, because somebody has to be looking for them, don't they?" For the first time she could see the ray of hope.

"Exactly," he agreed, with a smile. "So, if they've gone and messed with the British government, MI6 is bound to be all over it."

Smiling, she settled back some. "How the hell am I supposed to find somebody to fall in love with when I'm locked up like this?"

He laughed. "Like this, you're not," he replied. "You wouldn't want to fall for any of these guys, but you could start right now and make up a list of all the things you want in a partner. We have nothing to do here, so why not manifest a partner."

She groaned at that. "*Manifest?* Really?"

"Yes," he muttered. "Manifest. You want something, and it's not there. So you'll have to create it."

"*Great.*" She rolled her eyes.

"Come on. You've got nothing better to do anyway, so sit there in your mind and create exactly what you want for a partner."

She snickered. "How about somebody who loves me for starters."

He looked over at her, and his gaze was sad. "It breaks my heart to hear you not even realize that is a given," he muttered. "That is an absolute must, and you don't even know it."

"Why would I?" she asked, looking at him. "Pierre's idea of love was apparently beating the crap out of me."

"Yeah, and you wouldn't let me go after him either," Johnny complained, a sour note in his tone. "Admit it. You wouldn't let me get close enough."

"How could I? In the state you were in, you might have hurt him."

"Please don't tell me that you still care for him," Johnny moaned.

"No, but I didn't want you to go to jail either."

He chuckled. "I appreciate that you were looking after me, but somebody needs to look after you too."

"It hasn't happened so far," she stated, "and now I don't know if it ever will."

"Hold that thought. Somebody out there is looking for us, and we won't give up yet."

She smiled at that because giving up was one thing but completely losing hope was too much.

"You got nothing better to do, so close your eyes and start imagining your dream man."

"Is that what you did with your wife?" she asked in a teasing voice.

"Somewhat. I meditated and spent months trying to define what I wanted in a partner, and then, when she walked into the room, I recognized her."

She stared at him. "Seriously?"

"Yep, seriously." He laughed. "I know you don't believe me. I know you don't think it's even true or even possible, but that's because you've never fallen in love yet."

"Everybody talks about it, and I thought I was in love, but—"

"No, that wasn't love," Johnny argued instantly. "No way that was love, but that doesn't mean you don't have good things coming to you in terms of love. Trust me. Plenty of people are out there who will love you."

"You think so?" she asked sadly. "You get to the point

where you think something's seriously wrong with you. I always think that it's me. I'm the one at fault."

"That's because of what that asshole made you feel, what he told you over and over again," Johnny explained, "and that's unfair because it's not true. Lots of people are out there for you."

"Maybe," she muttered. "But …"

"Yeah, no more *buts* or *maybes*. That's the problem with you. It's all *buts*."

She laughed. "Not quite," she protested. "I'm not so foolish as that. I'm much more scientifically oriented, which is why what you're saying completely surprises me."

"But I'm French," he added, "and we love to be in love and to love. I didn't want to be in love with multiple people. I wanted to find the one true love. If you give it time, you will find someone."

"Sure, and that's great," Sammy hedged, "but finding that *one person* is a whole different story."

"Exactly. That's why I said that it will take time. Be patient and think of it in a very scientific way."

"There is nothing scientific about manifesting your life," she muttered.

He burst out laughing. "That's where you're wrong. You're the one who doesn't understand energy and how what you put out comes back to you. That when you do something good, it comes back to you, and, when you do something bad, it comes back to you as well."

"In that case," she said, "these assholes have a hell of a lot coming back to them. I only hope I'm around to see it."

"You will be," Johnny stated, with conviction. "Don't worry. You will." And, with that, he closed his eyes and repeated, "Now go do your homework."

She chuckled, then closed her eyes and started to picture what she thought would be a perfect man, but she had to stop because she'd never even seen a perfect man. She didn't even know what that meant. "I don't have a clue, Johnny," she cried out. "I can't imagine what he would look like. I don't even know where to begin."

"Stop thinking about physical attributes," he pointed out. "It's got nothing to do with the way he looks. Start thinking inside, who is he on the inside."

And, with that, she closed her eyes and tried again.

TERK LOOKED UP from the computer in front of him. "Interesting," he murmured.

"What's interesting?" Tasha asked, getting up to walk over and to look at his screen, only to then gaze at him.

"I'm getting an energy signal off the British agents."

At that, Wade joined them, placed his hands on Terk's shoulder, and said, "Boost it."

Terk closed his eyes and, using some of Wade's energy, gave a clipped nod. "They're alive."

At that, Wade dropped his hands, then stepped back. "So, we have a second part to this op, I presume."

"We sure do," Terk confirmed, clearly pondering the situation. "I'm not sure Jonas knows they're alive."

"So, do we get more money for that?" Sophia asked, from beside him.

Terk turned toward her.

She shrugged. "It happens. We find them their men, so a little bonus is thrown in there. Something extra seems right, correct? We should get paid for the extra duty, whether we can save them or locate them for Jonas to rescue."

"I can bring it up with them. Pretty sure they think their agents are gone though."

Just then Jonas called him. "Update?"

"Not a solution as yet," Terk replied, then hesitated. "The two MI6 agents who were over there …"

"Yeah," Jonas muttered, his voice dark. "No sign of them."

"No bodies though, right?"

"No, no bodies. That's the only thing that's keeping us hopeful."

"No ransom demands, nothing?"

"No, I wish there were, but these assholes are playing things close to the vest."

"And if they start killing MI6 agents …"

"Yeah, there'll be open war on that one," Jonas declared, his tone deepening with anger.

"What if we find them?"

"If you find them, there's extra money in it," he replied.

Terk grinned with satisfaction, looking over at Sophia. "There is some registering of energy, suggesting that they might be alive," Terk explained, "but I'm not sure for how long."

There was silence at the other end, then Jonas exploded, "What?"

"Yes," Terk confirmed. "I'm not too sure on the details yet."

"You find out and find out fast," he snapped. "Give me a location, and I'll get a team over there. French or English, I don't care who gets them out. We need those agents back," he stated urgently.

"Yeah, I know, and you also need the hackers back too."

"We do. Come on, Terk. I need answers, not just suppositions." And, with that, he hung up.

Terk looked over at Sophia. "We need more on the building that they're being held at," and he gave her the address to look into. "That—" Just then his phone buzzed.

"Hey," Riff began, sounding exasperated, "we have a couple complications."

"What's that?"

"We have an address from the asshole ex-boyfriend who saw Sammy being kidnapped. It didn't take much, as he caved quickly. Only it's a big warehouse district, and I'm getting more heat signatures than I like."

"You and me both," Terk shared. "I'm thinking the British government agents might be in there as well. If they are, and the kidnappers have any idea that's who they have, they'll go first."

"That's possible, but if we can stop it—" Riff paused, then added, "We found a USB key from one of the hackers and have it uploaded. I'm sending you all the details. A couple main warehouses are here in France. See if you can give us a rundown and choose which might be the better of them. Not sure if you got somebody on tap there who can do that, but I'm getting buzzes off two warehouses."

He gave him which ones to check. "I'll head out with the guys. We'll check the first one on this list that's giving me a buzz but forward any intel you have. Anything would be helpful." And, with that, he hung up.

Everybody scrambled to their computers, as the information hit their phones, one by one. Wade stepped up behind Sophia. "When he says that he's getting a buzz …"

"Yeah, so one of the things Riff can do is sense heat signatures," Terk confirmed.

The women looked at him, and then Sophia whistled. "Now that would be useful."

"It would, indeed." Terk nodded. "But it just means that he's getting heat signatures on both of these addresses, and that could be for a lot of different reasons, especially if they're warehouses." Terk brought up the maps. "Okay, so this is the first one that they'll hit." Terk tapped the monitor. "Don't know if it just seemed the most likely or something else."

"Call Gage and see," Sophia suggested.

But they didn't have to because Gage called them almost immediately. "Hey. We've just sent in a request for the cops to come pick up two burglars we caught in Sammy's apartment. It's her ex-boyfriend, and she had a restraining order against him. She also had a hiding spot in the wall. Plus, I've got a name for you."

"Who is it?"

"It's the partner she was working with, and I believe it's our other kidnap victim. Also, there's another name that I got out of the ex's mind. I'm hoping, with all of this together, you can make some headway on figuring this out."

"Yeah, Riff just contacted us and gave us the contents of the USB."

"Good," Gage replied. "We're heading to the first place now. I'm just going down the stairs. They're outside waiting for me."

"Hurry up or they'll be on the road without you."

Gage snorted at that. "I wouldn't be at all surprised. I can't say that we're exactly working in sync yet. Why would you ask for Radar? It appears he has no idea how we work."

"That's fine. There's a reason he's called Radar. His instincts are very solid," Terk explained. "We'll get back to you in five." He hung up, and his phone rang again. "Godammit," he muttered. He answered it, while he clicked away on the keys. "Hello."

"Where is he?" It was a hard female voice. "Where the hell is Riff?"

Terk stiffened, then looked around the room, before asking her, "Why are you looking for Riff?"

"Because he's ducking me," she snapped, "and that won't wash."

"Why is that?"

"Because it's my sister who was killed, and he's on the hunt. I want in. He keeps dodging me."

"That's nice," Terk replied cautiously, wondering at the powerful energy coming through the phone. "Have you talked to him about it?"

"I would if he ever talked to me, but he's determined to keep me out of it."

"Maybe that's because it's dangerous."

He heard her breath intake and then she declared, "You better not say that a second time." Her voice was ever-so-gentle, yet maintained a thread of steel at the same time. "A lot of women don't like being relegated down to the little missus."

"A lot of women," he clarified, his own voice equally hard, "don't understand that timing matters."

"Believe me. I can help Riff. Now, if you are in charge, and I think that's obvious, we need to talk."

"Why do we need to talk?" Terk asked.

She snorted. "Because I'm a pediatrician, and, boy, have you got some problems." And, with that, she hung up.

Terk stared down at the phone and shook his head. "My life is just way too crazy."

Sophia asked, "Did I just hear what I thought I heard?"

"I don't even know what I heard," Terk muttered. "Somebody is looking for Riff and is pissed off because Riff is trying to keep her sister's killer away from her or some such thing, or at least information about her death, and then something about being a pediatrician."

At that, they stared at him in shock.

"Oh my God."

"What the hell?"

"I'm not even going there," Terk replied. "No. … Let's focus on what's at hand."

And, with that, everybody tried to work on the mess in front of them.

"Got something," Tasha exclaimed. "The first address appears to be an actual functioning warehouse, but the upstairs was rented out for a separate business. However, that business went broke, and the place is supposed to be empty. The police were notified that there was an awful lot of activity that was fairly suspicious on that second floor."

"Good, so relay that information to the guys," Terk stated.

She quickly sent off messages to Gage. "Could we be so lucky right out the gate?"

"Hopefully."

"We need to see the file of the complaints or talk to those who made the complaints. Possibly both," Wade suggested. "Give me the number, and I'll go do that." And, with that, Wade stepped off to the side.

Tasha looked over at Sophia. "A doctor would be good," she whispered.

Sophia rolled her eyes. "Like we need one of those."

"But she's a pediatrician, and, with all the babies coming, we could use her. Do you think she's … an energy worker too?"

"I have no clue."

"If you'd stop talking and focus on the task at hand, we might have a chance to get some work done here." Wade openly glared at them. "As for the other question, yes, she has energy and a very strong energy at that." And, with that, he got up and walked out of the room.

The two women looked at each other and then burrowed back into the work.

Wade returned and said, "I got a description from the warehouse bosses down below. Two people were led in a couple days ago and two more yesterday. One's tall. One's skinny."

"So, that could be our hackers and the British agents," Sophia pointed out.

Wade nodded. "It's a pretty good chance I think." He turned around, frowning. "Where's Terk?"

"I think he's probably prepping for an unannounced arrival," Tasha suggested. He now frowned at her, and she shrugged. "I don't even know what I mean by that."

"Hey, you're getting good at this though," Wade noted. "No, you really are."

"Send that message off to Gage, will you?" With a half smile, she turned back to the computer.

"On it," Wade teased.

RADAR HOPPED OUT and looked up at the building that spanned more than half of the block. "This would take a bit to get into." Just then his phone rang. "Wade, what's up?"

"Radar," he acknowledged, "we have intel on the building you're about to go into."

As he listened, his gaze went up to the second floor. "Now that's interesting. We'll start there." With that, he hung up, as he headed over to Gage. "Apparently the main floor foreman reported strange activity on the second floor, which was rented but is supposedly no longer occupied. A couple people were led in there a couple days ago and two more yesterday."

And, with that, Gage nodded. "I'll stay in the truck."

Riff gave him a nod in return. "I'm taking the back."

Radar stared at them both. "That leaves me the front."

"Your cover?" Gage asked.

"Don't need one," he muttered. "I'll think of something when I get up there."

And, with that, the men split up. Radar eyed Gage as he headed to the vehicle. Radar could use some backup. But then he had Riff onsite, and Riff was obviously full-on backup material. He didn't seem to be bothered by Gage going to the truck either.

Yet Radar felt something very strange going on here. He raced upstairs, and, as he got to the door, he noted that Riff had entered from the other end of a long hallway between them. The front wall was all windows, facing the street, but doors were off to the other side on an internal wall in this hallway.

Riff motioned at the first door, and he turned the handle, but it didn't open. He pulled out tools and quickly popped the lock. Stepping inside, he came back out; his thumbs-down motion had both Radar and Riff going door by door. When they came to the one big double door in the center, they heard a voice in there.

Riff stepped back, just as the door opened.

Two men stopped partway in full conversation mode. "We still have to make decisions, but, if they don't know anything, they're just dead weight."

"We must find out if they shared the information."

"What a shit show from the beginning. They were snagged from us before we even had a plan in motion. These two came in prepared, so what if more come?"

"Yeah, but two of our men died in that process," the other man snarled. "They'll pay for that."

"Sure, we can take out the two MI6 guys, but then we have to disappear. What are we doing with these two hackers? If they're that good at their jobs, can't we use them ourselves? Bribe them to be on our side?"

"No, better we make sure we have copies of all the information and then just deep-six them."

"I want to take out the two MI6 guys. That one gave me a hell of a punch to the head, and returning the favor wasn't enough."

"It's not that simple though. We can't bring MI6 down on our heads."

"None of it's simple. However, we need to update the bosses, follow their orders," he said, a note of disgust in his voice.

At that, they walked out of the doorway, one going left, one going right. Radar stepped up in front of closest guy, gave him a big fat smile and a right hook. The bad guy dropped soundlessly. Radar looked over to see that Riff had done exactly the same thing. They peered down through the open double doors and saw a large room with several other doors.

They dragged the two unconscious men back inside.

"Check the rooms. The first empty one can house these morons for now."

They dragged them in there, and Radar pulled out zip ties and secured their hands. As Radar and Riff raced down the hallway from one room to the next, they found the two MI6 agents on the floor, both tied up together and blindfolded. They quickly released them, but both were in rough shape, having been worked over hard. Radar pulled out his phone and quickly called Gage.

Gage spoke before Radar could. "I know," Gage confirmed. "I've got an ambulance coming for them. Leave them where they are and see if you can find the other two hostages." Gage disconnected.

Radar stared down at the phone in shock. "He knew?" He shook his head and quickly moved to the next room and the next. In the last room were two civilians, curled up in the corner, trying to sleep. He bent down in front of the woman. "Sammy?"

She bolted upright, then fell from the ties on her legs.

Radar cut the ties and quickly helped her get stabilized. "Hey," he murmured, "it's okay. I'm here to rescue you."

"Oh, thank God," she whispered.

He quickly cut the ties at her wrists.

"They're coming back," she said hysterically. "They said they would come back to talk to us. I got the impression that we had to talk or we wouldn't like what happened next."

"Nope, I'm sure you wouldn't," Radar agreed, as he helped her take a couple steps, wincing as she stumbled.

"My feet aren't working so well," she whispered.

"That's okay." Radar scooped her up in his arms and raced from the room with her.

She turned back. "What about Johnny?"

"My partner has him." Radar pointed to Riff, already with Johnny.

Outside in the hallway, she said, "Put me down. I can walk."

"Are you sure?"

"Yeah."

Radar nodded. "Okay let's go. Our priority is to get you two out of here."

"They've got other prisoners," she muttered, as he raced her forward and down the stairs.

"I know. We'll go back for them." With Johnny in tow, they were quickly ushered outside to the truck. Radar put her into the back seat, hopping in on the other side. Then, with Johnny in the front seat, the vehicle pulled out, and Radar hit Gage on the shoulder. "Wait, wait. ... Riff isn't here."

"I know," Gage replied. "He's staying with the MI6 agents, waiting for the ambulance."

"Shit, but he's alone."

"He'll be fine."

"How do you know that, man?" Radar roared. "I don't like leaving anybody behind." At that, his phone buzzed. He pulled it out, and there was a text from Riff.

Don't worry. I'm fine.

Radar sat back and whistled slowly.

Gage looked at him in the rearview mirror. "As I said, he's fine."

Radar looked over at Sammy beside him. "Here, rub your hands together." She stared at him oddly. He picked up her hands and started to rub them. "It will get the circulation going. Your legs too. Here. Give me your feet."

Twisting her sideways, he grabbed her feet and started to

massage her ankles.

"Are you always like this?" she asked, with a half laugh.

He frowned at her. "The sooner you feel better, the sooner you'll realize you're okay and safe. It's just basic human kindness," he stated gently.

She nodded. "And I appreciate it very much. How is Johnny?"

"Johnny is fine," Johnny responded from the front seat. "I'm grateful for the rescue. That's not where I wanted to spend any more time."

"No," Radar muttered. "We heard them talking about what they would do to both of you and the government agents."

"Which is why I presume Riff stayed behind?"

"Exactly."

"I'm grateful," she muttered.

Radar saw her tears welling up. "It's been a hell of an ordeal, hasn't it?" he asked gently. She nodded in understanding, but a sniffle escaped. He pulled her close. "I'm sorry," he whispered, "and I'm really sorry to tell you that we found your ex, tearing apart your apartment."

She reared back to stare at him in anger. "Seriously?"

Radar nodded. "Yeah, so we very nicely called the cops on him. I hope you don't mind."

She slowly shook her head. "That asshole," she muttered. "Johnny," she called out to the front seat, "seems you were right."

"Yep, I was." He turned to face her to give her a nod of satisfaction. "That's definitely not the guy for you. Of course you look to have done much better this time."

She stared, not knowing what he was talking about, yet afraid that she did. She muttered to Radar, "Don't worry about him. He's just … French."

At that, Radar laughed. "My name is Radar, by the way, and I understand the French are very different when it comes to relationships."

"Nope," Johnny disagreed. "We just don't waste a lot of time on the wrong ones. She did. She didn't want to be alone, so she wasted time with Pierre."

"Hey, that's not fair," she argued, clearly embarrassed.

"That's another thing about the French," Johnny added. "We don't get embarrassed by love."

She sighed. "Johnny, we've been friends for a long time, but sometimes you are still completely foreign to me."

"No, I'm not," Johnny clarified. "You would just prefer that I didn't talk so plainly."

"That would be nice for once," she muttered. "At least if you didn't embarrass me all the time."

Johnny chuckled and turned to face the road.

She smiled at Radar, teary-eyed. "I don't know who you guys are or how you found out we were missing, … but thank you."

"Thankfully, when you were snatched out of the back of the lorry at the tunnel entrance," Radar explained, "you were seen. Then the vehicle's license plate was caught on camera. The vehicle was burned after you were taken out of it, and then we found out your dearly beloved had a good idea of who took you."

"The people who took us and the ones we left with were not the same."

Radar nodded. "It appears that you were kidnapped by the very one you've been tracking."

She sat back and stared.

He nodded. "Frenchie."

"Oh my God," she whispered. "We never had a picture or a face, not confirmed, not one we could count on."

"That was him, and your dearly beloved ex-boyfriend knew who it was. Although I can't know for certain that Pierre knew him as Frenchie."

"How is that even possible?"

"I don't know, but he did. Maybe he'd seen pictures of him somewhere along the line."

"We had old photos," Johnny noted, confused, "but nothing current."

"Maybe Pierre was approached. Or maybe he broke into your place and searched your data. Maybe we need to have another talk with the ex-boyfriend," Radar mentioned to Gage.

"That's a good idea. Let's do that now." And he quickly changed course, driving them in the direction of the police station.

"I don't want to see him," she cried out. "I don't want anything to do with him."

Radar replied, "In that case, I'll stay here with you, and Johnny and Gage can go talk to him."

And that's what they did. As soon as they disappeared into the police station, she chewed on her bottom lip to the point that he reached over and gently rubbed her lip with his thumb.

"Hey you're damaging your lips. Relax. It'll be fine."

"No, you don't understand. Pierre is just … he's one of those shitty people, and it makes me so angry that I've let him do this to me."

"Then let's go in there and face him," Radar suggested. "Nothing like facing a monster to see what he's really like. He may have mistreated you, but he's here in jail, where he can't hit you now."

"But what if he ever gets free again? It's just a burglary charge, and he'll be out in no time. Then he would come after me."

"Maybe," Radar said, considering it. "How did he know about your little hiding spot?"

"Because I was stupid enough to not be careful around him. One day he saw me put something in there."

"Then what did he do?"

"Beat me up until I told him what it was," she admitted.

"So, if he knew about Frenchie, maybe he put out the word that you had something."

She stared at him in shock. "I wonder—"

"Let's go talk to him," Radar said, and she shook her head. "Listen. I know you're scared. I know this guy has beaten you up, and he's filled your sleep with nightmares of how to get free of him, but that's not the way you want to live going forward. You don't want to always look behind your back to see where this guy is."

"No, I don't," she agreed, "but, at the same time, I don't really want to go in there and face him."

"What if he had something to do with this? What if he's the one who told Frenchie what you had?" She stared at him, the color draining from her face. He nodded. "Don't you want to go in there and find out once and for all?"

She swallowed. "Can I hit him?"

He laughed. "As far as I'm concerned, you can. So, yeah, and, if it makes you feel more in control, more like you have control over your life, … absolutely." With that, he hopped out, walked around to the side, and opened up the door of the truck for her.

"Will you come with me?"

"Hey, I've got no better place to be. I'll stay with you every step of the way," he noted comfortably. "I don't do well with bullies."

"Yeah, but you're a guy," she said.

"In general, bullies ..." he began, looking down at her, "go after weaker vulnerable people because they don't put up any fight. Bullies can't handle any real fight. They're cowards."

"Maybe," she whispered, "but ..."

"No, it's okay. I'm not trying to make you feel bad. Guys like him are all over the world. It's just how it is. But we can stop this one from coming after you."

"Do you think so? Because nothing I've done so far has stopped him. And even the restraining order didn't make any difference."

"No, they tend not to, and unfortunately they're only good if somebody follows the rules. This guy didn't follow the rules right from the get-go, so why would he now?"

Her shoulders sagged, but, as they headed into the police station, they caught sight of Gage coming out.

"Oh good," he said. "I was hoping you'd come in."

She looked up at him. "Why?"

"He wants to talk to you."

She winced. "I don't want to talk to him though."

"Maybe not," Gage acknowledged gently, "but he's not quite so intimidating now." She frowned at him. "I gave him a bit of an extra kick for you earlier at the apartment. He's a little on the bruised-up side."

"I wish I'd done it," she stated.

"Nobody says you still can't." Gage laughed. "Believe me. I'm very much of the opinion that you're much better off to take charge and to beat your own demons than to sit on the sidelines and let other people handle it."

She winced at that. "Can Radar come with me?"

"Absolutely." As he looked over at Radar, his lips twitched. "You didn't have a girlfriend back home, did you?"

He shook his head. "No, why?"

"Nothing, just checking."

Radar frowned at him. "Dude, we need to talk. You guys always seem to know stuff I don't."

"That's all right," Gage responded. "I heard your own radar was pretty good."

"It can be, yeah, although you guys have thrown me off my game," he admitted.

"Maybe you should get back on it."

"Why is that?"

"Because of her," Gage said, with a laugh.

And, with that, they were led into another room, where Pierre sat handcuffed to a chair. He took one look at her, and he leapt to his feet. She walked over, and, with her fist pulled back, she slammed it hard into his jaw and sent him reeling backward.

"You ass!" she screamed. "You see me get kidnapped, and, instead of calling for help, you go ransack my apartment? As far as I'm concerned, you're right in the middle of this."

One of the cops reached out an arm to block her second punch, as another cop set Pierre back up in his chair.

Speaking to her in French the cop said, "Tell us what happened."

And, with that, she switched to French as well.

Radar understood enough French to get by but not enough to sit here and to follow the spat that was now going on. As soon as she started talking, Pierre started arguing. By the time it was done, he was looking much more dejected and curbed.

"Is he clueless or what?" Gage asked. "He recognized one of the men who kidnapped her and decided to contact him, looking to make some money. The guy told him that they were looking to find any information she had on Frenchie, and that's when lover boy here came to the apartment, and we happened to find him. So, the idea was that, instead of getting her free, he would give up the information."

"For what? What was he getting out of it?" Radar asked.

"Money," Sammy snapped. "He wanted money so he could leave and have a fresh start somewhere. He wasn't even trying to bargain to get me back safely." She snorted, looking over at him.

He had the grace to look ashamed at that. "It was obvious you didn't want me. You put up that ridiculous restraining order."

"Really? And you hadn't just proven again how dangerous you are to me?" she cried out.

He shrugged and didn't say anything.

At that, the conversation was hard and heavy, as he was forced to give up the name of his contact person, how that guy then contacted Frenchie, and what it was that Pierre was doing. At that, Radar looked over at the cop and said, "I presume we have more charges involved than just breaking into her apartment and destroying property."

The other guy looked at him and nodded grimly. "Yeah, he won't be getting out anytime soon."

"Thank heavens for that," Sammy declared, looking over at Pierre and glaring. "I hope you rot in prison, where you get beat up daily too." And, with that, she stormed out.

Radar quickly followed her. Outside the door, she

stopped and leaned against the wall, then buried her face in her hands. "Dear God, how could I have been so stupid?" Almost immediately she was wrapped up in warm arms. She looked up to see Radar staring down at her.

"You did good. Not only that, but, because of what you did, we now have a lot more information, and Pierre can be charged with a felony. He can spend a whole lot longer in jail. I'm really proud of you. Not only did you do that for yourself but you did that for your future."

She looped her arms around his neck and gave him a big hug. "Thank you, and thank you for rescuing me and for helping me go in there. As a matter of fact, it's really just … it's a thank-you for saving my life."

He smiled. "You're welcome, but it's all good."

CHAPTER 4

AFTER A FEW moments, Sammy stepped back and smiled. "Can I go home now, please?" She was staring at him, with a besieging look.

He frowned at that request. "I have to check in with my bosses on that. We don't have details on what's supposed to happen now." She winced. "Not to mention"—he reached up a hand and brushed the hair off her forehead—"I think you need to be checked over by a doctor."

"I'm fine," she said. "Honest to God, I'm fine."

Johnny spoke from behind her. "No, she's not, and, yes, we both should probably get checked over."

She turned and glared at her friend. "Or we could just go home, right?"

Johnny just stared at her and then at Radar.

She looked from one to the other and asked, "What am I missing?" She knew her brain was quite confused and messed up after everything that had happened, but it was obvious that the two of them were thinking about something she hadn't considered.

"The problem is," Radar explained, "you were found once, so what's to stop them from finding you a second time. Going home isn't an option."

All the heat washed from her face again, as she looked at him. "Good God, you don't think they'll be done with us?

Why? I don't get it. We're not that important."

He smiled. "Did they get what they wanted?"

She frowned and then shrugged. "Maybe."

"Maybe?" he asked, with an eyebrow shooting up. "How can there be a maybe with this?"

"Yeah, maybe. I don't know. They were talking about wanting me to show them how I tracked the bomb maker, so they could make sure that he was never found. Either to keep him safe or themselves, I'm not sure which, or whether that's an issue or not."

"But they didn't get the USB key," he noted. "We've got that, and chances are good they'll just go back after you, if they want more info."

Her shoulders sagged. "So, will I be on the run for the rest of my life?" It was a sucker punch to the gut. She stared up at him, her gaze going from one man to the other. "And what about Johnny's family?"

At that, Radar looked at Johnny and said, "About that, I think it is time to relocate."

Johnny nodded. "Yeah, you're not kidding, and honestly my wife has been talking about it for a while. I need to get them picked up, before somebody else does."

Radar pulled out his phone. "Give me the address. Will they be at home? Where do you want to move to?"

Johnny hesitated, then he looked at Radar and said, "I would prefer to do it myself. Unless there's a reason why you need to do this."

"Nervous much?" Sammy looked at Johnny. "You were talking about the Netherlands. Are you still?"

"Yeah. Plus it would be nice to think I could get some of my work from there. Like Sammy, I saved a bunch of it, but I can't afford to have anything go wrong with my family."

"Got it," Radar replied. "In that case, why don't we go with you?"

Johnny studied Radar. "I really won't get much chance to do this on my own, will I?"

"It's not that we're trying to cause trouble for you. You may need to speak to the government who asked us to come and rescue you. I don't know, but I do know that I can't just let you go free. However, if your family is potentially in danger, we need to pick them up, but we need to do it together."

"And take you straight to my family?" Johnny asked bluntly. "We don't want to go from one hostage situation to another."

At that, Radar faced him. "My orders were to come rescue you. I don't take hostages, and we sure as hell don't play around with the lives of children."

Johnny gazed at him searchingly for a long moment, and then his shoulders relaxed. "I don't know whether I should trust you or not, but I believe you. My wife went with the kids to her sister's place for a few days. It's part of the discussion we were having about our future." He turned and looked at Sammy. "I didn't even tell you about it."

"No, you didn't," she said. "Were you about to leave everything?"

He shrugged. "Or at least move somewhere that wasn't so dangerous. You'll remember that we did talk about it a couple times."

"We did," she agreed. "We just didn't get as far as making any commitment either way."

"No, but I guess my instincts kept saying that we needed to move, to get away, and this right here? This just proved it."

She winced at that. "I won't argue with you on that. We've just gotten freed from a kidnapping, which I hadn't really seen as being in our future. Yet obviously it's something we should have thought about."

"And it's something you still need to think about." At that, Radar moved them both toward the vehicle, as Gage stepped forward and said, "Let's go. Time to move."

With them ushered into the truck—Gage and Johnny in the front seat, with Radar and Sammy in the back seat, she asked Gage, "What's this got to do with anybody here? Can we relocate? I don't understand. Are we your prisoners, or maybe not that bad, but I feel like we need your permission to do anything."

"I'm not anything other than what I said I am," Gage replied. "I have MI6 on the phone right now. They apparently need to talk to you."

She groaned at that. "They wanted to talk to us before, but I can't say we were terribly open to the idea."

"How do you feel about it now?" Radar asked her. "Because they're the ones who hired us to come get you."

"Yet we were kidnapped while we were with their other agents, so it's not as if they have great security either."

"Neither does it inspire any confidence," Johnny pointed out.

"Which is why we now have our own men going to your sister-in-law's place to pick up your wife and kids. They'll get them safely to England on their own, and we can always discretely send a moving company back to get any of your belongings."

In the back of the vehicle, Sammy looked over at Johnny. "They already have my USB key." He looked at her, then switched his gaze to Radar, who nodded.

"We got it from her place."

"In that case," Johnny admitted, "you have exactly the same material I had hidden. I made two copies."

"What got you two onto this pathway?" Gage asked, from the front of the vehicle.

Sammy watched the road, as the miles just seem to fall away, her life once more out of control. She had no idea where they were going. She listened as Johnny explained about his uncle, and the other man seemed to understand. She certainly had, and it had gotten her on board this special project with Johnny. Also her need to have something important to do, something that meant more in life. She'd been idealistic, not realizing the danger.

And now that she did know more about the inherent dangers, she wasn't sure she wanted to change a thing. At times you just had to pick a side, and Johnny had been a friend for a very long time. They'd met at their university many years ago, and, through his marriage and the birth of his two kids, that friendship hadn't changed.

When they finally headed into the tunnel, she sank back into her seat and muttered, "I still don't understand what a lot of this is about. Why does everybody care? I get Frenchie's associates don't want the tech getting into MI6 hands, but you have the USB key, so why do you care how we did it?"

"Because other countries are all tracking that bomb maker too," Radar replied. "And they may not have your information. I gave it to my bosses, not MI6 directly."

She nodded. "But the government should have more sophisticated methods than we do."

"Maybe, but you've hit upon something that's making everyone very nervous."

At that, she slowly turned and faced Johnny and then focused on Radar again. "Do you know what that is or in what way Frenchie or his kidnappers communicated that?"

"No," Radar admitted, "except for the fact that they have tried repeatedly to get you into their clutches. We need to put a stop to this and ensure you guys are safe. To do that, we must get whatever information they seem to think that you have. That's dangerous, and frankly I'm a little amazed that you're still alive," Radar shared. "You have to understand that, for terrorists—like Frenchie, this bomb maker, and his kidnapping buddies—another death is absolutely nothing."

Radar looked over at Johnny and added, "As you well know, lots of deaths occur in terrorist attacks such as this Frenchie enables. His bombs pack a big punch and aren't selective as to who they kill."

Johnny slowly nodded. "Yeah, I do know that." Johnny looked out the car window. "Ever since my uncle died, I've been quite obsessed with tracking down this particular bomb maker. We finally got to the point of being able to do that quite efficiently and accurately each time. Then we contacted the French government. That was apparently a stupid idea, and look what happened."

At least there was no rancor or blame in his tone, and that was good.

SAMMY WASN'T SURE she had the same lack of blame in her mind as did Johnny. She sensed Radar studying her features. She looked up at him and smiled. "Yeah, what he said."

Radar continued to stare at her, and she shrugged.

"Johnny and I have been friends since college, and, when he jumped on board this bandwagon, I joined him. No reservations because I knew his uncle, and what happened to him was terrible, and I didn't want it to happen to anybody else."

"Did you specialize in computers in college?"

She smirked. "Yes, but we were gaining more hacking experience out of university than we were learning in classes." She shrugged. "Once you start accessing all this stuff that most people don't know how to do, there's a certain amount of freedom—a freedom that becomes addictive."

"Have you ever done anything illegal?" Radar asked her.

She shook her head. "Not in the sense that you mean, so no. We don't hack into bank accounts. We don't steal money or data. We don't sell personal information, nothing like that. We were trying to find this Frenchie guy. And then, this happened." She stared over at Johnny, who sat almost numb in his seat, staring out the truck window. "Please let us know when his family has been picked up," she whispered.

At that, Radar nodded. "I will." Suddenly his gaze narrowed, and he leaned forward to Gage and said, "Watch out for the right-hand side."

Gage didn't say anything, just gave a quick nod. He quickly checked all the gauges on the dashboard and then pushed an odd button on the vehicle.

"What does that do?" Radar asked Gage.

"It's kind of like a deflector, so we become a much brighter image out there. I put it on when I was waiting for you guys earlier."

"What do you mean, you put it on?"

"It's just a reflective screen."

"Now why would you want to bring more attention to

us?"

"It's not so much bringing more attention to us, as much as anybody coming our way now realizes that to do anything would bring attention to them."

"Frenchie and his kidnappers can't really do anything here," Sammy stated, then hesitated. "Can they?"

"There are ways, yes," Gage replied, "but we're not going there right now." He looked over at Johnny. "If we get separated, you stay with me." Gage looked back at Radar. "You got that?"

"Not a problem," Radar agreed easily. "You get Johnny. I've got Sammy."

She frowned. "You make it seem almost guaranteed that we will get split up."

"Not guaranteed, but definitely possible," Gage confirmed.

"Where's Riff now?" Radar asked Gage.

"He's got the government agents and going on a completely different route."

Radar nodded. "So he got out of there with them?"

"He did."

"That's good," Radar said.

"But will he be okay? Alone? Surely he needs backup?" she asked. "The kidnappers were pretty adamant about the punishment they would dish out, if we didn't cooperate."

"I'm sure they were," Gage agreed, with a smile. "They must threaten you in some way, right?"

She sank back, restless, but sensed that the men were waiting for something, making her far edgier than she wanted to be. "It wouldn't be so bad, but you guys don't relax," she cried out into the darkness of the vehicle.

"We can't afford to right now," Radar explained, his

voice calm, steady. "You never know when an attack is imminent, and you have to be ready for anything."

As it was, they made it out of the tunnel and up onto the other side. As soon as he had a chance, Gage gunned the vehicle and raced forward, heading into a series of constant evasive maneuvers to keep anybody behind them off their trail.

"Jesus," she muttered, as the vehicle swerved off the freeway at the last moment. "Are you sure that's what you want to do?"

Gage nodded. "Yep. It absolutely is."

"I presume they have satellite," Radar noted. "So, it's smart to assume we've been tracked the whole way."

"So, now what will you do?" she cried out softly.

"We'll get you to an inside meeting place, where you're safe."

She gave a broken laugh. "You're making me think I'll never be safe at this point."

"There *is* a safe place," Gage stated, "but it might take a minute or two to get you there." Another series of maneuvers ensued, as they raced into London. However, they were headed into an area that she'd never been, even though she'd spent a fair bit of time exploring. They were in a commercial district. She couldn't even read the street signs, as they were flashing by so quickly.

When Gage took their vehicle into an extreme hard right, then another left, followed by another right, she hung on with all her might, even while she was tossed from side to side. Radar put out his arm and pulled her up against him, holding her close.

Gage ducked the vehicle into an underground area and came to a sudden stop.

As the rear passenger door suddenly opened beside Sammy, she cried out when someone quickly shifted her into another vehicle.

She was freaked, but the calm confidence oozing from the two men assigned to keep her and Johnny safe gave her strength and a weird sense that they knew what they were doing. The next trip was way shorter, before they pulled into a large secure parking area and then were led upstairs into the building. "Now where are we?" she whispered.

"MI6."

RADAR KEPT A hand on Sammy's shoulder, knowing that she was getting nervous. "It'll be fine," he said.

She stared up at him and then shrugged. "Nothing personal, but it hasn't been fine yet."

"I get that," he noted gently, "but you didn't have me at your side then either." He flashed her a wicked grin. "Since we've met, things have been great."

She sighed. "It's really not fair that you have those disarming dimples and that you should be this cute."

He looked at her in surprise and then burst out laughing. "I'm not sure there's anything fair or not fair about any of this," he replied, "but it's definitely not a game to us."

"I'm glad to hear that," she muttered in all seriousness, "because it would be upsetting if you thought your looks and charisma are … all part of some game."

He shook his head. "No, definitely not. It's also not something I take seriously."

At that, she chuckled. "Yeah, well, not everybody has won the looks lottery."

"Maybe not, but you definitely did."

Startled, she looked up at him and frowned. "That's probably one of the nicest things anyone has ever said to me, especially considering how I probably look right now."

He snorted at that. "Honey, if you haven't heard that before, then you don't know the right people."

At that, Johnny looked over at her and chuckled. "I've been telling her that for ages, but she hasn't been very good at listening."

She protested, "*Hello.* I'm right here, you know? So not exactly oblivious to your conversation."

"Well, since you *are* part of the conversation, I would hope not," Johnny quipped. "Remember what I said earlier?"

"I'm not sure which part of what you've recently told me is important, but it sure seems as if there's always an awful lot more that you're saying but not exactly making clear."

He rolled his eyes at that. "You keep believing that. You're getting closer, but I don't think you're close enough."

She sighed. "You could try making things less cryptic."

"Come on. Given the work we do, how would that work out?"

She smiled. "You're the one who tells me that you want me to find somebody special and to let go of the guys who are like that idiot Pierre," she muttered. "But then you won't come out and say what you're truly thinking."

He gave her a mischievous grin. "I'm afraid you'd be very embarrassed if I did." And, with that, the door opened beside them, and they were pushed into a large hallway and through a set of double doors.

Gage looked over at Radar, who, not wanting to give anybody on the other side much warning, pushed open the double doors and stepped inside. A group of men stood nearby, talking, and they turned to see who the newcomers were.

Radar grinned at Jonas. "Bet you never thought we'd make it, did you?"

The relief that washed over Jonas's face as Johnny and Sammy both walked into the room was unbelievable. He looked at Gage. "You did it," he cried out.

Gage nodded. "Yeah, and a little more notice would help, but—"

"We never get more time," Jonas declared. "Generally this is the way of our world. Hard and fast. Something you should expect."

"Just thought you could try it for a change." Gage looked over at the other men with Jonas and studied them carefully.

Jonas smiled. Didn't introduce them.

"Now, the next question is, where do you want them?" Gage asked.

Before anyone said anything, Sammy spoke up. "What do you want us for anyway? How about we start there?"

"You already know that," Jonas replied. "We're trying to track the bomb maker."

She shrugged. "Yeah, and apparently other people want that information too."

"Exactly, and you had some of it put away, I believe."

"Yes, but we've also got a copy of it now," Radar stated, holding up the USB key.

At that, Jonas's face really lit up, and he held out his hand. "Now that is what I need." But Radar held it back and away. "Oh no you don't."

Jonas snapped in astonishment, "No games."

"No, absolutely no games at all," Radar confirmed, "but

we need to ensure that these two people are safe from here on out. Obviously whatever measures were taken last time didn't do the job."

"We know that now," Jonas muttered in frustration. "We've already found a mole in our department, and we've closed that loophole. Whatever you've got for information on tracking this bomb-making guy, we need it because we have solid intel that he's setting off a bomb in London."

At that, Sammy gasped and stepped back slightly. "Let me have a computer," she said urgently. "I can see if there's been any change to the algorithm I worked up."

Jonas stared at her. "Can you track Frenchie in real time?"

"No, not exactly real time," she clarified, "but I've been trying to get ahead of him. I had figured his next target was either London or Paris. I'd bet that the destination shifted from Paris to London because Paris was so abuzz with you guys and a lot of their men, so it shifted. Johnny and I were working so hard on this, and, of course, Paris is also where we live."

"*Lived*," Jonas corrected. "I understand your place was trashed."

She winced. "Yes, and apparently my incredibly stupid ex was trying to get the USB information so he could sell it to the bomb maker's group as well," she shared. "I'm not responsible for the crap he did."

"Got it," Jonas replied. "Come on this way." He quickly led them to a series of offices and pointed out the closest computer desk. "You can have that one."

She sat down, then reached back to Radar for the USB key, and he put it into her hand without hesitation, then stepped up behind her. "You do you," he said. "I'll be right here."

She beamed at him. "You really are a nice man, aren't you?"

He winced and she laughed.

"Right, Johnny would say that would be the last thing I should tell a guy and that being nice doesn't exactly raise your personal status, but it really does work for the rest of us," she noted, with a smile.

"Yeah, I never did quite understand that," Radar muttered. "Since when does nice work?"

"When there's not a whole lot else in the world to work with. So nice works just fine for me."

Beside her, Johnny sat down at another computer, and, as soon as she copied over the key, she handed it to him. With the two of them working, Radar looked back over at Gage, who was on the phone talking, so Radar pulled up a chair and sat down beside Sammy.

"I can't believe you developed this," Radar admitted in amazement. Although he knew an awful lot of great hackers were out there, it was something to watch Sammy's and Johnny's skills at work. Their fingers danced across the keyboards, as if they had the ability to power all kinds of things. And Radar didn't have any clue what that was. Speaking of powering and what he was thinking of, he walked over to Jonas. "Have you heard from Riff?"

At that, he looked up, smiled, and nodded. "Yes, he's at the hospital with our two agents," he murmured. "You guys did great. The first time out of the gate, and you guys absolutely knocked it out of the park."

"Glad to hear that," Radar replied, then headed back to stand beside Sammy. Yet, even as he stood here, he got a weird tingling sensation. There really was a reason for his nickname, *Radar*, but he'd often found that, when he needed that tingly sense, it wasn't there for him, particularly when other things distracted him. So he headed off and sat close to the window and closed his eyes, waiting to see what would pop up.

Usually he just called it his instincts, yet there had to be a reason for the tingling right now. Whether it was set off by what Gage had said about Riff or something else, Radar didn't know, but something was off. At this stage of the game, when something was off, it was bad news.

He opened his eyes to search around the room again and then closed them again. Gage and Jonas were on the phone, which was to be expected. However, Radar was looking for a whole lot more than phone calls out of these two guys. Something else had to be happening, per his tingly sense, but he just didn't know what it was. As he sat here, his eyes closed, he then opened them to stare at the third man in this room, who was on another computer, working away, same as Sammy.

Radar got up, walked over to Jonas, waited until he was off the phone, then nodded backward at the man working. "Who is he? What is his job, and what's he doing right now?" he asked bluntly in a low voice.

Jonas frowned at Radar. "He's one of us. He's been verified, and I assure you that he's definitely not the enemy. I presume he's helping us track down this Frenchie guy."

Radar didn't like anything about that answer because he didn't like anything about the vibe he was getting off this guy. He casually walked over and around him.

The guy switched screens, then looked up at him and glared. "I don't like anybody behind me."

"No, maybe not," Radar stated, "but I want to ensure

that everything here is aboveboard and that these two don't have to go through any more hell than they've already been through."

The guy looked at him in astonishment. "I'm on your side—in case you haven't figured that out."

"I haven't," he declared, giving him a feral smile. "So don't mind me while I continue to check what you're doing to confirm."

At that, the guy looked back at Jonas, who shrugged and said, "Just keep working, Andy."

He shrugged too and kept on going.

This time Radar saw the screen. Not that it made a whole lot of sense. He was good with computers but not anything on the level these people were at.

Just then, Gage put away his phone, then turned toward them.

"I see you guys are getting the handle of this game pretty damn fast," Jonas noted.

"We have to," Gage said. He called out to Radar. "Hey, Riff is at the hospital with the other two, and we've delivered the hackers as per our agreement."

Radar looked at him, and his stomach clenched. "You're thinking that it's time to leave?"

Gage studied him for a long moment. "And you're thinking it's not?"

Immediately Radar shook his head. "Nope, something is going on, and it'll get ugly." He made a slight motion toward the one guy on the computer behind them.

Gage instantly transferred his attention to the guy that Jonas called Andy. Then he turned and looked back at Jonas. "What computer is he using?"

Exasperated, Jonas repeated, "Look. I've just told Radar

here that Andy's been cleared. Everything is fine."

"Maybe it's fine with him, but it's not fine with that computer," Gage snapped.

At that, Jonas stared at him, shocked. "The computer?"

"Get him off that computer."

But before they could do anything, all the screens in the room went dark, as if they had suddenly lost internet or power.

"Shit," Sammy cried out. "What the hell was that?" She glanced over at Johnny, who was staring at her in shock. She turned and looked at Jonas. "What happened?"

But Jonas didn't have an answer for them.

Radar headed right for Andy. "Andy, what did you do?"

He stared at him. "I didn't do anything, godammit. I'm not a part of this," he muttered. "Take your suspicions elsewhere."

"No," Gage confirmed, "it was this computer."

"How the fuck do you know?" Andy asked.

Radar looked over at Johnny and Sammy and asked, "Can you guys fix it? If it's on this computer?" They both raced over to check what was going on.

When Radar tried to say something, he got shushed. He groaned, then stepped back, looked over at Gage.

"You're right," Gage confirmed. "Something is off."

"Yeah, you may want to alert the others. It's not a danger to them, but definitely something is going on here."

At that, Jonas joined them. "What did you just say?"

Gage nodded. "Something's going on *here*. That computer was responsible for what went down just now," he explained. "You've got a hacker in your system, and they're trying to get whatever it is that Sammy's just uploaded."

"Which means they must have known that she was

about to upload it," Jonas muttered.

"Or they have a trace for our signatures," she suggested. "Given that they tracked us down to my apartment, that's possible."

Radar and Gage shared a look, and both shrugged. "Maybe update our other half," Radar offered.

Gage nodded. "I already did, but you're right. Something's going on." He turned to face Jonas. "How secure is this building?"

Realizing that they were well past the point of joking, Jonas frowned. "This is our best security systems."

Radar added, "We can expect visitors at any moment."

Jonas glared at him, but Radar smiled. "Hey, I'm not necessarily here to be a pain in the ass, but I am the one who alerted you to that computer."

Jonas shook his head. "I still don't know what could be wrong with that computer." He frowned at Andy. "Did you sense anything wrong with it?"

Andy shook his head, without hesitation. "No," he said, looking bewildered. "I don't even know how it could have been something on that computer."

"Is it connected to a mainframe here?" Radar asked.

"Sure, they all are," he replied, "at least once you put in your password."

At that, Radar added, "Doing whatever you did has triggered it. Just bringing up that computer may have been enough. But then they must have known that we were here and that we would be using these computers."

"Yes, but hacking into the system isn't all that hard," Sammy muttered.

At that, Jonas protested. "Hey, hey, hey, this is a secure system." At that, both Gage and Radar just smirked at him.

Jonas raised both hands in mock surrender. "Fine, we always considered it a secure system, but obviously we have to rethink that now."

"You do," Radar stated, "because you've been compromised. The questions are, how much did they get, and how much damage will they do? They may be doing it right now, and what will we do about it?"

"*You* don't need to do anything," Jonas replied, with a knowing smile. "We do have our own cybercrimes unit."

"That's great," Radar said, "but you're not keeping these two people if you can't keep them safe, and, so far, this isn't keeping them safe."

Jonas glared at him. "Your job is done," he snapped.

"It is. I delivered them, but I'll also take them out of here, if that's the way this game gets played," he snapped right back. "I didn't bring them over here to set them up to be patsies. So, if you can't protect them, I will."

Jonas looked over at Gage, one eyebrow raised, but Gage was already nodding.

"I agree with Radar. We don't do a job, then just put the people we rescued in more danger."

"They're not in more danger," Jonas argued in exasperation. Just then an alarm went off in the building, and he started to swear.

"Yeah, and how about now?" Radar muttered.

Jonas glared at him. "Are you guys armed?"

"Yes."

Startled, he eyed them both.

"Of course we are," Gage noted, "but they aren't."

"No, and that's a good thing," Jonas said. "Look. I want you guys to stay here, while I go check this out."

"Okay, but you can bet that nobody had better come in

here without us having a full visual and knowing we can double-check that they are with you," Gage declared. "Otherwise, no way in hell anybody is coming in, at least not without being shot."

Jonas looked at them and nodded. "So, you'll keep Johnny and Sammy safe?"

"Yes," Gage confirmed, "but take Andy with you."

Jonas turned to Andy and motioned for him to come.

Andy protested. "But then we're leaving these guys alone with the computer systems."

Jonas sighed. "Where do you think they are now, with you right here?"

He winced. "Fine," he muttered, "but the bosses won't like this."

"You'd be surprised what the bosses can get used to," Jonas replied, as he looked back at Gage, with a final warning. "Keep this aboveboard." And, with that, he was gone, and they were alone.

CHAPTER 5

S AMMY RACED OVER to Radar's side. "What's going on?"
She spun around, clapping her hands over her ears as
the alarm continued to sing throughout the building. She bit
her bottom lip to stop it from trembling.

He reached out, grabbed her hand, and spoke into her
ear, "The place is under attack."

She stared at him. "An MI6 facility? Surely that's not
possible. Isn't this at least physically super secure?"

He looked at her grimly. "It is. However, it's annexed to
the main building, and apparently somebody seems to think
that whatever's here is worth coming after."

She felt everything inside her tremble. "You mean, such
as me and Johnny?"

Radar nodded. "Yes, apparently so. Make sure you have
copies of that USB key, just in case we are under attack." At
that, he turned and looked at Gage, who nodded.

"I'm taking Johnny with me. We'll take the right."

Radar nodded. "I'm taking her with me. We're heading
to the basement."

With that, the two split up. Radar grabbed her hand, not
giving her a choice in the matter, then pulled her out of the
room and steadily down the hall toward the stairwell at the
far end.

"Why split up?" she asked.

"Because it's easier to hide two than four."

She shook her head at that. "Who's hiding who though?"

"That's the question. We like to have options. If they find a better way out, we can follow them afterward."

She had to trust Radar, but it was hard. "Why not just find a dark empty room and hole up there, until all this is over?" She was wondering out loud, still keeping up the killer pace. Her heart slammed in her chest, as reality set in.

He smiled. "Stick with me. I'll get you out of here."

"Yeah, says who? You think we haven't already been jostled around like a sack of potatoes, or maybe I should say, like the last sack of potatoes on earth."

He burst out laughing at that, and, just as he swung open the door to the stairs, he stopped, frowned, and shook his head. "Not that way." Then he headed off to another set of stairs.

Surprised, she could only follow helplessly, as he dragged her with him. "Why this way and not the other way?"

"Instincts."

Well, damn. She'd never thought about that. "Are instincts really a big part of what you do?"

He tossed her a surprised look and nodded. "Isn't it for you?"

She frowned, thinking about that. "I guess instincts are just an inner knowing that we need to go left, and we shouldn't go right, *huh*?"

He laughed. "Or instincts that tell you that, even though you're going left, you really should change course, and go right."

"Is Radar really your name? Do you have some strong radar sense or something?" she half joked, but she studied his features intently.

He shrugged. "I can sense danger coming. Just put it that way, and, yes, it's my nickname."

"That's a hell of a good kind of instincts to have," she murmured. "Is it okay that Johnny and Gage went the other way?"

"Yep, as it is. … Besides, their way didn't work out, and they're heading downstairs too."

"How do you know that?" she asked.

He flashed her a grin. "Instincts."

She groaned. "Or is that just what you would do?"

"That's what I would do."

"Okay," she noted, "I can accept that."

He laughed. "It's a good thing, if you think about it. A lot of things in life we don't know. Except Gage seems to have some sort of … I don't know, *silence* in his world, as if he's doing things we can't see or hear."

"Maybe he's just super quiet and very introverted."

"All of the above, except I don't think he's introverted. He's … let's just say he's very smart and operates on many different levels." He was already pulling open a door but yet in a stealthy way, as if he already knew it was safe somehow.

She frowned at him. "Are you sure about this?" she asked.

He nodded. "Come on. Let's go." He pulled her forward, tucked her inside the door, and came in behind her into a utility access room, now taking the back door out of there.

"Where are we?" she asked, as he quickly took the lead and started running flat-out to the end of the hallway.

"We're in one of the maintenance tunnels," he replied, "underneath the building."

She shook her head. "How did you even know it was here?"

"Instincts," he replied, with a cheeky grin.

She shook her head. "We'll have to talk about these instincts of yours."

"Sure, over a bottle of wine maybe," he offered, as he waggled his eyebrows at her.

She had to laugh, even though nothing was amusing about their situation. "You're just trying to keep my spirits up, or are you always this fun-loving, footloose, and fancy-free person?"

"I'm not sure I'm any of those," he admitted, "but, right now, not a whole lot of purpose in getting upset over this. We know where we are, and we have a good idea who is after us. Thus, with those kinds of answers under our belt, we can do a lot."

She shook her head. "You might do a lot. I just want to curl up in a ball and cry."

"Yeah, that never really worked for me," he said, with a serious note to his voice. "I'd much rather get the hell out of Dodge, before anybody can get a hold of me."

"I agree with you there. I just wasn't expecting to be running through the basements and the tunnels."

"What do you need in order to get the information you want?"

"Back to the same computer would be nice. Any chance of heading back there and holing up?"

"No, we'll have to find another safe place. But that's all right, we'll get one."

"Are you sure about that?" she muttered. "Seems we're all over the place, anywhere but safe."

"True, but that's not where we'll stay either," he noted.

"I wanted to get you out of that building, while everybody is taking care of the problem."

"And will they take care of it?"

"Sure, but what we can't be sure of is whether it was a serious security threat or mostly a distraction, so that somebody could get to you."

"But then, following that logic, doesn't it make sense that the distraction was to make us run?"

"Yeah, absolutely it is, which is why we are running but not toward them. We'll be a long way away from them."

"Are you sure? It doesn't seem we're going anywhere very quickly."

He chuckled. "Come on, girl. You gotta have a little faith."

She decided to stop talking because he set a brutal pace. When he finally came to another door, she gasped as she collapsed against it. "I hope it's locked." He frowned at her. She shrugged, grabbing at a stitch in her side. "It would take you at least five minutes to open it, and I could catch my breath."

"You can catch your breath later," he stated. "Really no time for it now." And, with that, he had the door open in half the time she'd expected.

She stared at it and groaned. "I thought I was in shape."

"The trouble is, when you're running from something like this, you can't keep your breathing under control, due to anxiety and pressure, so you use up too much oxygen. You get a stitch in your side, and you very quickly wig out. It's just a simple matter of pacing yourself."

"That's great logic and all," she muttered, "but I can't say I really want to be in a position where that becomes useful."

"It *is* useful," he stated, giving her a mocking look. "Just think about it. You could have used that information a few minutes ago."

"But I still would need to be in a position to make good use of it, and right now I'm not feeling like doing that."

"Maybe not." Radar shook his head. "Come on. Let's go." Then he pulled her in through the doorway.

"Are cameras in here? Will anybody follow us?"

"I don't think so. I didn't see any as we came through."

"Doesn't mean they aren't there," she argued.

"Nope, it sure doesn't. It does mean that we have a much better chance here."

"What about the others? I don't want anything to happen to Johnny."

"Of course not," Radar agreed, "but that's Gage's problem."

"Says you," she muttered. "At the moment, anything to do with any of us seems to be all one big problem."

"And that's a really good thing to keep in mind," Radar said. "This has become an all-hands-on-deck deal, and it'll take all of us to get to the bottom of it."

"I just don't understand why Frenchie cares. If he's out there, setting up more bombs, what does he care about us tracking him or not?" Radar again frowned at her, as she shrugged and went on to explain. "Think about it. He'll just change his pattern, and then what? I'll be set back again."

"But, if you could do it once, you'll do it again, and that's what he's trying to stop."

She pondered that and then winced. "I suppose I was just thinking that we could hand off this information to somebody who could go after him, and then we'd be free and clear."

"Yeah, I don't think that belief system will work out for you."

"It certainly isn't working right now," she admitted. "I'm really worried about Johnny's family too."

"A team was instructed to pick them up, so let's hope that got done."

"I hope so too, and once we get free—" All of a sudden he opened the door to fresh air and sunshine. She gasped in shock at the suddenness of the outside world. "That already feels a whole lot different."

He grinned at her. "Right? Nothing quite like feeling a sense of freedom and being out in the open."

"Yet somebody could also see us," she noted, as she peered outside.

"Potentially, but I'm hoping that won't be the case here."

She shook her head. "You're doing an awful lot of hoping. I'm not sure I agree with it."

He chuckled. "Life's too short to worry so much. It took me a bit to figure out what was going on here, but, now that I'm in the game, it's all good."

"Why is that?"

"Because I don't normally work with Gage and Riff," he shared, "but being adaptable helps."

"Yeah, and yet it's funny," she replied, studying him. "You have that same look to you."

"What look is that?"

"A look of surety and secrets," she said. "A look of somebody who knows something that nobody else knows, somebody who's got skills that other people don't really understand." He stopped and looked at her, as she shrugged. "It makes no sense, right?"

"I don't know. It makes a lot of sense to me," Radar replied.

He spoke with that same cheerfulness that she was wondering about too. How could he always be so happy?

"At the same time, this isn't the time to talk about it," Radar added.

"No, and, with you, I don't suspect it will ever be the right time."

"What do you mean by that?" he asked curiously.

"I just think that, in your case, there will always be something else to talk about."

"Meaning that I won't be boring at least. I like the sound of that too."

She laughed. "Again, you're sending out all these vibes that it's no big deal."

"What's the big deal?"

"All of this is a pretty big deal to me."

"Don't ever think that I'm not tuned in to how serious this is," he clarified. "However, it's more than that. ... It's more about making sure we're on track for where we need to go."

"Yeah, but you don't even have any place set up for where we're going," she cried out.

At that, he pulled her back from an upcoming corner to the building and held a finger to her lips. She hadn't seen or heard anybody, but he had. His ear tilted toward the corner, his eyes closed, he was waiting for something. She watched him intently, and then he opened his eyes suddenly and smiled at her. "It's all good."

She let out her breath slowly. "Says you."

"We're going up to that vehicle ahead."

She noted one parked off to the side, as if somebody had

come to work and had parked it there for the day. Lots of other vehicles were around, so she wasn't sure why he was focused on that one. "Any particular reason why that exact one?"

"Yeah." Radar nodded. "Instincts."

She sighed. "That instincts response will get old real quick."

"I hope not," he teased, "because there's an awful lot left to use it for later."

She pondered that, as they headed toward the car. She thought it would be locked or at least it should have been locked, but he very quickly gained access and unlocked her door as well. He pulled out his phone and quickly sent a message. He turned to face her. "We'll pick them up in a few minutes."

"You mean, if they can be picked up."

He shook his head and smiled. "You have so little faith." She sighed again, just as his phone buzzed, and he gave a nod of satisfaction. "Five minutes." And, with that, he turned on the engine and headed around to the front of the building.

And, as casual as one can be, out walked Gage from a side door with Johnny. They walked over to the car, hopped in, and Radar took off.

She twisted to look at Johnny. "Are you okay?"

He nodded. "I'm fine," he replied shakily. "How about you?"

"I'm fine," she said. "I still don't quite understand how or why though."

Johnny chuckled. "I'm not sure any of us do at this point, but they're just trying to keep us safe."

"I had no idea that it would become so unsafe."

Johnny nodded. "And, for that, I'm sorry. I guess that's

probably more my fault than yours."

"How do you figure that?" she asked curiously.

He shrugged. "I knew what I was getting into when I started this. In your case, you were just along for the ride."

"I was hardly an innocent in the whole venture," she protested. "I was working with you every step of the way."

"Still, I don't think that you really were prepared to die for it."

She winced at that. "I was really hoping it wouldn't come to that, actually."

Johnny smiled. "I'm still hoping it won't come to that."

When Gage's phone rang, he answered it very quickly and hung up after just after a moment. "Your family is safe, Johnny."

The immediate look of relief on his face made Sammy realize just how worried he'd been. "I'm really glad to hear that," she said, "but what are we supposed to do now?"

Gage recited an address, and Radar punched it into the GPS.

"What is that?" she asked, looking bewildered. "Where are we going?"

"It's likely a safe house," Gage shared. "That's a pretty important next step."

"A safe house? Does the government just have a bunch of those hanging around for no purpose?"

"The purpose is for people like us right now," he explained. "So they definitely have a purpose."

She winced at that, "Okay, fine, but … is this safe? This safe house?"

"Yes," Gage replied, "at least for the moment."

She watched as Radar very quickly navigated through the streets according to the GPS, avoiding minor skirmishes anywhere along the line in traffic. They ended up pulling into a single-car garage, which automatically closed behind them.

She twisted to look around at the interior of a normal-looking residential garage. "This is it?"

"This is it," Radar confirmed.

The interior door to the house opened, and there stood Jonas.

She stared at him. "So, this was always a backup plan?" she asked cautiously.

"One of many," Radar pointed out. "Believe me. We always have contingencies. Plan A, B, C, D, E, and, if we need it, we can create more on the spot."

Feeling somewhat better, she scrambled out of the car and headed over to Jonas. He smiled at her. "Glad you got out of there."

She showed her palms, shaking her head. "How is this even possible? That was supposed to be a very secure area."

"It was," Jonas agreed. "Don't worry. We're looking into it."

"Yeah, well, I'm not sure that's an answer that I can really live with right now," she muttered. "It seems to me it should have been a whole lot more secure than it was."

At that, Jonas chuckled. "You're probably right, but you're here, and it's all good. Back there, everybody else is still looking for you."

She frowned and looked over at Johnny. "I guess we need to get to work." She turned back to Jonas. "If you've got computers for us."

"Oh, I've got computers for you," he replied cheerfully. "I've got an awful lot of people waiting to hear what you come up with."

"Great," she muttered, "nothing like a little pressure."

"You saw what it's like now, and we can't assume that you weren't followed. So, the sooner you get at it, the better for all of us."

Not much to say to that, so the two of them headed inside, finding computers already set up and waiting for them.

Andy stood off to the side.

She frowned at him.

"Yeah, this is something we deal with on regular basis," Andy stated.

She sighed and shook her head. "Better you than me." Then she sat down at the first computer but quickly looked back and stated, "I need food, and I need coffee."

"Coffee is coming up," Andy said, as he headed to the kitchen. "We can get some food together too."

"Good," she replied. "I also need to change clothes and to get a shower." She felt disgusted at the lack of basic care they had endured all this time. Nobody seemed to make any comment about her demands, though even Johnny sat down beside her with a grin that said it all. "Sorry, but that's just the way I feel," she admitted, with an irritable shrug.

"Got it. Now let's get some work done. The sooner we do, the sooner we can get out of this mess."

"Do you think there *is* any getting out of this mess?" she asked, as she quickly brought up the pages she needed.

"I do," Johnny stated. "Just make sure you're keeping everything hidden."

"Yeah, I've already set that up," she replied. "Plus, of course, we're under observation. Therefore, everything we do keystroke-wise will also be counted."

He chuckled. "Can't say as I blame them."

"Maybe not, but, at the moment, I'm not feeling too

generous about any of it."

"Well, get over it," Johnny declared. "This is what we're here for, and, after all, we did contact them, even if they ignored us."

She winced at that and nodded. "I guess that's our own fault then, for contacting the French government to begin with, isn't it?"

"No, it was what we needed to do," Johnny admitted in a hushed tone. "Keep that in mind. There'll always be some things in life that go our way, and others that don't. But this is what we had to do. Otherwise, we would be in even bigger trouble."

"I guess," she agreed. "You just don't really realize what'll happen when you make that phone call and say, 'Hey, we've got a problem,' right?"

"It is what it is. We did it, and here we are, lucky to be alive. So we better make the most of it. Now let's just get the job finished, and I can consider what I'm doing with my family."

"When you say *consider*, what does that mean?"

"Salina's brother wants us to move back to the Netherlands."

At that, Sammy raised her eyebrows. "Wow. ... Then why not? You've spent a lot of time focusing on this, and, once it's dealt with, it's a good idea to start fresh."

"That's what I was thinking," Johnny confirmed. "I've spent an awful lot of time getting to this point. I want to ensure that we finish it successfully. Afterward I need to realign some priorities."

"Anything in particular?"

"No, just the fact that I haven't put my family first, and I need to. Nothing like having this blow up in your face to make you realize it's something you need to reassess."

"No, I get you there," she replied. "Family is every-thing."

"It is when you have family. In your case, maybe it's easy to ignore it, but I don't know about that. For me, it's always been about family."

"Got it," she noted. "Let's just deal with this, so we can take care of whatever needs to be dealt with afterward." And, with that, they both bent their heads to the task.

When the cup of coffee arrived at her side, she didn't even acknowledge the server, just picked up the cup and started sipping at it, as she worked. When a plate with a large sandwich arrived beside her, she munched through that as well.

When she finally sat back, groaning because her back was hurting, she got up and adjusted the height of the chair and started to stretch. Then she realized that all the other men were just sitting around, watching them. "You guys don't have anything better to do?" she asked suspiciously.

"No, you tell us where we're going, what we're doing, and we'll be there," Jonas explained. "In the meantime, we're here to look after you."

She nodded. "We're close. I've picked him up in Paris, which is a first."

He looked at her and asked, "Where?"

At that, Johnny answered, "He just used one of his alias-es and a credit card at an apartment." He quickly gave Jonas the address.

"When you say an alias …" Jonas began.

"We've tracked six of them so far over the last few months," Sammy supplied. "He just triggered one of them."

"Is this something you would expect him to do, or do

you think it's more along the lines of a trap?"

She frowned at him, contemplated the question, and then said, "I would expect him to use them at some point. This is one we haven't seen put to use yet, so it makes sense that it would be one he's pulling out now."

At that, Jonas spoke into his phone, as if to set up some op.

"Remember. If you get there too fast, and you blow his cover, we won't be able to track anything after this. And this could just be somebody else or an accomplice." Radar reminded him when he was done.

Jonas nodded. "We'll head over and take a look, but that doesn't mean we'll jump in."

"Better not," she warned. "Because if you lose him at this stage ..." He glared at her, and she shrugged. "Just saying."

"How about you just keep on working?"

She shrugged. "I need more coffee, and I need another sandwich. While you do that, I'll have a quick shower and clear my head." She looked at Johnny and asked, "You're good for five?"

"I'm good for five," he confirmed, "and I'll have a shower after you."

She headed to the bedroom and noted one of her bags sat on the bed. She frowned, stepped outside, and asked, "Who went to my place?"

"I did," Radar replied.

She looked at him in shock. "After me asking to go there and turning me down, saying it wasn't safe, you went there anyway?"

"I didn't tell you that it wasn't safe. I stated clearly enough that it might not be safe. I just went in, grabbed you some clothes, and came right back out."

"You really don't think you were seen?"

"I'm pretty sure I wasn't seen," he stated, with that same dimpled smile.

She sighed. "I sure hope you got me some comfortable clothes."

"You had an abundance of leggings and T-shirts, so I figured that was your work outfit."

"Yeah, that's pretty close."

"Sounds about right," Johnny added, at her side. "I don't think I've ever seen her in anything other than that."

"That's enough out of you," she muttered, then headed into the bathroom, locking the door behind her. Inside, she quickly turned on the water, checked out what Radar had brought, and realized that he hadn't done too badly. He even packed multiple changes of underwear, bras, T-shirts, leggings, and a sweater to curl up in.

She wondered how he'd known that these were her favorite clothes. But, then again, he seemed to know a lot of things that she didn't really understand. After a shower, she brushed out her wet hair, then braided it and spun it into a single bun, but then decided it was better to let it dry down the center of her back. After brushing her teeth, she felt marginally better and headed out to find a sandwich waiting for her at the computer, along with a fresh cup of coffee.

"Wow, what service," she said.

"If you can get it, that is," Jonas replied. "However, it's not unlimited."

"No, of course not." She gave him an eye roll. "We really are working, you know?"

He just silently stared at her.

She sighed. "I guess showers don't come into your world

of work, do they?"

"They do if they have to," he admitted. "But, if they don't, it's all the better."

"They have to for me," she muttered. She sat back down again and, with fresh eyes, opened up her module, logged back in again, and checked on another variation of the name that had occurred to her while she had been in the shower. As soon as she brought it up, there was another hit. "Found a second apartment under a variation of that same name."

Johnny leaned over, took one look, and nodded. "That's quite possible too."

"What's the variation?"

"His father's name. His father is dead. Doesn't mean there aren't another dozen people with the same name, mind you, but, in this case, it is an apartment and only one block away from the other one."

"So, are these long-term rentals?" Jonas asked. "Why would they do that?"

"No, these are short-term. It's booked for a week." Then she gave him the address. "You should put that one under observation as well. At least until you know who's there."

"Yeah? We don't have unlimited man-hours."

"Nope, neither do you have unlimited citizens to get blown up."

At that, he shut up.

She didn't say anything else, but Johnny looked over at her with a smirk. "The shower didn't help much."

"Sure it did," she argued. "I was snappy, and now I'm really snappy. I wasn't thinking this had become my life."

"No," Johnny acknowledged, "and I'm sorry for that."

She waved her hand. "None of that crap either," she said. "We're in this now. Let's just get the hell out of it."

And she got back to work.

RADAR STEPPED OFF to the side and called Terk. When Terk came on the line, Radar began, "Not sure if you've had an update yet or not, but we have some interesting developments." He quickly filled him in and added, "I'm not sure whether I'm supposed to stay or not."

"If I told you to leave, what would you think?"

"I would think we are deserting them when they need us," he replied.

"Does that sit wrong?"

"Of course it sits wrong," he said in exasperation. "You don't need me to tell you that."

He chuckled. "No, I sure don't. Also, there is the fact that she's there."

"What about her?" Radar asked hesitantly.

"I'm getting the idea there's a connection."

"So what?" he replied in disgust. "And don't you start that crap with me too. Levi's gone over the top with the matchmaking."

"What's to start? There is no need, since I can already see the energy."

At that, Radar stopped and then swore heavily. "From there?" he asked in exasperation.

"No such thing as time or distance when energy is concerned. You know that."

"I'm not sure I know any of this," Radar admitted.

"Stick around, and you'll learn soon enough."

"And if I don't?"

"Then you won't. We all have our gifts, specific to each

one of us. It's just that simple."

Radar groaned. "Levi did warn me that some weird stuff was going on with your team."

"Are you staying with Levi?"

"No. I'm still on the move because I haven't really found where I want to be."

"Let me know how you feel about this job, after we're done."

"Why?"

"Because we're always looking for more people with a built-in radar system." And, with that, Terk rang off.

Radar stared down at the phone, then started to curse mentally. The last thing he wanted was for anybody to think that his *radar* was anything other than plain-old instincts. Going down that pathway would only bring misery. He quickly sent Terk a text and told him exactly that.

Terk sent back a thumbs-up, which revealed absolutely nothing, yet at the same time said so much.

Radar groaned, as he stared down at it.

"It's nice to know that it's not just me who reacts that way to Terk," Jonas noted in a conversational voice at Radar's side.

"The man is definitely interesting," Radar acknowledged, shaking his head. Then he looked over at Jonas. "What about your recovered agents? Are they able to talk yet?"

"They're both still unconscious in the hospital, under guard," Jonas replied.

"Right." Radar then looked around, wondering where Riff was. He quickly sent Terk an message, asking for an update on Riff.

He got back a somewhat terse message, saying Riff was

looking into another aspect of the case. Radar frowned, as he put away that thought.

"What was that about?" Jonas asked suspiciously.

"I asked for an update on Riff," Radar shared, "since he was the one who took your agents to the hospital, but I don't know where he is now."

"Good point. Last I knew, he was at the hospital, and I presume he checked in with Terk."

"He did. I was just looking for more of an answer as to whether he was coming here, so I could potentially leave to go off and do something else."

"What would you go off and do?"

"I'm more of a field type person. So, instead of sitting around in this room, I would do better on the outside."

At that, Jonas laughed. "I can relate. The trouble is, we're still looking for more avenues to pursue."

"Yet you have two addresses."

"I do. I have two addresses, and they're both very important, but that doesn't mean that either one of them would give us exactly what we need."

Radar frowned at that. "Maybe not, but, at the same time, we do need to know that they're being checked."

"They are. I just haven't had a report to say what kind of setup there is. All we have so far is the registration confirmed in those names."

Radar pondered that. "Okay, so that's something."

"Yeah, but it's not enough for anybody to go on. We need more than that, and we need this Frenchie guy taken off the streets, not just creating another bunch of aliases for us to track down."

"What gave you the idea that he was becoming another threat here locally?"

"He sent a message to MI6, saying that it was time we were taught a lesson."

"Ouch," Radar replied, "but that's also good in a way."

"What's good about it?" Jonas snapped, staring at him.

"That ego will get him into trouble. He had to announce his presence, which is a bad move on his part, even if it's a good thing for us."

"Everything this bastard does is a bad move," Jonas stated. "He has taken out way too many people with his bombs, yet people always cover for him, which I never quite understand."

"No, but really not any understanding to be had. Sometimes people are bribed. Sometimes they're forced to keep quiet, and sometimes they don't get a choice. They're dealt with afterward, as Frenchie just takes them out. So far, he hasn't left much in the way of tracks."

"So, then these credit cards."

Radar nodded. "Yeah, I would suspect that it's probably a trap," he suggested, looking at the two programmers, clicking their keyboards. "Yet I can't take a chance of not checking them out." Radar pondered. "Let me go take a look," he offered, watching Jonas carefully. "I'm a face they don't know. I'm not part of MI6, and, even if I pop up on a database, all kinds of reasons why I could be there."

Jonas sighed. "Anytime any of these groups that you're associated with come into my world, things get blown up, and I end up having to deal with a lot of bodies." He gave Radar a wry smile.

"Yeah, welcome to my world," Radar said, chuckling. "But the work we do is always of value, so, if you end up having to clean up a few places afterward, that's hardly an issue."

"Says you," Jonas muttered. "It's not exactly the easiest thing to convince the bosses of."

"No, but you also know that we do good work and that it's work that needs to be done and that can't necessarily be tied to you guys."

"That's half the problem. These bomb maker guys end up creating such chaos in our world that we end up stuck trying to figure out who was involved."

"As I said, let me head over there, and I'll take a close look at both apartments."

"What are you, some cat burglar?"

Radar gave him a fat grin. "Yeah, something like that." And, with that, he walked over behind Sammy.

She looked up. "What's up?"

"I'm going outside to do some reconnaissance," he shared, "unless you have any particular place to send me."

She smirked. "You were just waiting for somebody to send you somewhere, weren't you?"

"I sure was," he stated agreeably. "It's what I do."

At that, the smile fell from her face. "Good point," she noted crisply. "I don't have any particular place to send you to, but I've given Jonas two addresses. So use those instincts of yours and pick one. Of course they are both in France so a bit of drive for you."

"Yeah, that was covered already," he muttered, as he looked up at the window. Catching sight of a shadow moving by, he whispered, "Stay alert." Then he stepped over to Jonas. "I'll go take a look outside." There was no sign of Andy, and, for all Radar knew, Andy had gone out on a garbage run.

Jonas asked, "Anything in particular?"

"Nothing in particular but also nothing good. Something feels wrong."

And, with that, he stepped out the front door, stopped in the shadows of the garage, and studied the area. Something was definitely off, but he couldn't put his finger on it. He quickly shifted around to the back, where he'd seen the shadow, but found no sign of anybody moving out into the alleyway.

Heading down farther, he walked around the block, until he came back up on the other side. There he caught sight of somebody moving at a quick pace, even with his head down. Radar stepped into line behind him.

Once the guy looked up and around and saw him, he then accelerated.

"Gotcha," Radar whispered.

The man's pace had become nearly a full-out run, as he headed toward the corner of the block. Radar cut through a backyard and around the corner, where he picked up the pace and sprinted, hoping to cut off the guy, before he reached his destination.

As the man came around the corner and slid into the driver's seat of a vehicle, ready to start it, Radar opened the door and pulled him out onto the ground, before the runner had a chance to lock the doors.

The guy started screaming for the police.

Radar slapped a hand over his mouth. "Why are you calling for the cops? If you want me to take you to them, that's absolutely no problem. I'm sure they'll have quite a lot to say to you."

The guy just stared at him, wide-eyed.

Radar held him to the ground and quickly checked his pockets, only to find a piece of paper with an address on it. His fingers went cold, as he pulled out his phone and sent a message to Jonas that he'd found somebody with their safe house address on his person. **The place is compromised. Get everyone the hell out now.**

With the warning sent, and fighting his instincts to race home and get Sammy out, Radar got the guy back up on his feet. "Some people want to talk with you."

"Nope, nope, nope," he muttered. "I can't. No way."

"Yeah, well, it doesn't matter if there's a way or not," Radar stated. "These people *will* talk to you."

At that, the guy started to blubber. "You don't understand. I was just asked to look for an address."

"And? What about the address?"

"I was just supposed to check it out and see if anybody was there."

"Did you check in and give your results to the guy who hired you?"

He nodded. "Yeah, I did. Of course I did because they told me to do it as soon as possible."

"Of course. And why are you parked clear down here?"

"I didn't want to get caught."

"Yeah, so you're okay to set up a whole houseful of people for certain death, but you don't want to be involved, right?"

"For death? What do you mean?" The guy turned around and looked at him in shock.

Radar studied his face and groaned. "Are you really that stupid?"

"It was for one hundred bucks," he said. "It was like, … I needed the money."

"Of course you did. So, how did he find you?"

"I was just sitting at the pub around the corner. I had asked if anyone had any work. I needed the money, man."

"So, somebody offered you a job, right?"

"Yeah, just to come down here and see if anybody was in the house. Then wait for a few hours and see if somebody came or not."

"Okay, and when you found out that somebody was there?"

"I was to let them know, and then they asked me to stay there and to wait to see if anybody left, or came and went, but nobody did. It was just you guys."

"Us guys?" Radar asked carefully.

"Yeah, I saw you in the living room window once."

"Yeah, and did you take a picture of me?"

The guy swallowed and then nodded. "Yeah, they promised that I'd get extra money for it."

"Of course you did." Radar shook his head. "Guess what? Now you get to go meet the people in the house, and we'll let them know exactly what's going on."

"No, no, no. I don't want to be anywhere near that house, not now that I've told him that people are there."

"Oh, I know," Radar agreed. "That's exactly why you will. So, you can see the end result of your actions."

"No, no, no," he balked, pulling back hard on Radar's hold. "I don't want to go anywhere near there, man," he wailed, shaking. "Those guys were scary."

"Did they prepay you?"

He looked at him, then slowly nodded, "Yeah, he did."

"So, why the extra credit then?"

"Because he said there would be more money."

"Do you really think they'll pay you?"

He shrugged. "Why not? They paid me for the first job."

"Sure, but this way, you go back, and, when you do, they get to take you out."

At that, the other guy stopped in his tracks. "Are you serious?"

"Sure. They pay you for the job with the hundred. You don't worry about it, but you'll get more money if you give them more information. So, because you've already made an easy hundred, you can already count the rest of the money in your mind. Therefore, you try to find something extra, and now you need to meet up with them, right? So they can pay you."

"Yeah," he replied slowly.

"That becomes his opportunity to take you out. He got the information he wanted, and nobody knows anything, and he probably takes back his hundred."

"That's not how business works," the other guy protested. "Why would they want to take me out? Like, … I didn't do anything."

"But neither did we," Radar stated, his voice equally hard. "What you've just done is let him know that we are there for the attack."

"Yeah? So what? For all I know, it's his house, and you were breaking and entering."

"Or maybe we're law enforcement, and the guys who hired you are on the opposite side."

At that, the young man swore. "I just want to leave, man. I won't tell them anything."

"But you already have, right? So, if you don't check in for your money, then they'll know that you probably got made, or you lost your nerve. So, did you give them any idea where you lived or where you hang out?"

He stopped to stare at him, wide-eyed. "No, I was just at the pub."

"So, a little tip for you. I wouldn't go back to that pub if

I were you."

"You'll let me go then?" he asked hopefully.

"No, not until I take you around and let you have a little talk with MI6."

At that, his eyes grew wider. "Who?" he asked in a squeaky voice. "Man, I didn't know anything about that."

"But you didn't ask either, did you?"

"No, I was just looking for money for a meal, like … I haven't eaten today. I was just … I needed some money."

Radar almost felt sorry for the guy. "And the pub didn't have a job for you?"

"No, they weren't hiring. It seems like nobody is hiring."

"*Huh*. That's funny because I thought I passed a half-dozen signs up and down the road, all looking for help."

The guy swore. "Look. I just want to be left alone. I don't want any more trouble."

"You got yourself into trouble already, so that's really not my deal." Then he slowly walked him back toward the house.

As they got closer, the young man's feet lagged more and more.

"Yeah, you already know what'll happen when you get up there." Radar glared at him.

"Look. I don't know what these guys are doing."

"But you were okay to throw us to the wolves for whatever though, right?"

"I didn't know anything about it, honest."

"If you're honest about it, then it won't be an issue. Maybe nothing will happen, but we'll get you in the middle of that house, just so you can see for yourself."

"See what?" he asked.

"See what those new friends of yours do and see what a

mess you got yourself stuck in." As they walked up closer to the house, his phone rang. He pulled it out, nudging the other guy forward.

The guy took one look at him and said, "You could just forget about me."

"I could, but I won't. Gage, what's up?" Radar asked.

"We're out of the house, and I see you coming down the street. Who's that you are with?"

"The guy who sent out the alarm," Radar replied. "I figured Jonas might want to have a talk with him."

At that, Gage's phone changed hands. "That's the guy?" Jonas asked.

"Yeah, he was picked up, … chosen at the nearby pub. He was sitting around, and he'd apparently been asking for some pick-up work. Some guy paid him one hundred bucks to come and check out the building."

"You can probably let him go then," Jonas muttered in disgust.

"Maybe, except that will probably end his life, if I do."

At that, the other guy looked at him in shock.

"What do you mean?" Jonas asked.

"These guys offered to pay him a bonus, if he got some extra information. And, of course, he did, but now he has to go collect. So he's got to contact them."

"But if he does, that'll be the end of him, although we might use him to get to them."

"Yeah, and I told him that. However, if he doesn't want to contact them now, they'll have no trouble finding him again. If we track him back to the meeting place, we'll just see him be killed too."

"Right," Jonas agreed, with a sigh. "Head him down to me, and I'll think about it. An unmarked car is at the end of the block, a black sedan," he noted.

"Yeah, I saw it on my way out. I'll put him in the back."

And, with that, he kept on walking, until they got to the end of the block, and there was the sedan. He pointed at it and told the guy, "Better get your ass in that vehicle. Otherwise I'm not sure if you'll be around too much longer."

The guy swallowed and repeated, "I really just wanted a meal."

"I'll tell the guy in the car that. I don't know if it'll make any damn bit of difference or not, but we might keep you alive long enough for you to get that meal."

With that, he quickly hustled him into the vehicle. Then Radar headed down the road, back toward the house. As he got closer, he dodged into the backyard of another property, just as his phone rang again. "What's up?" he asked.

"What's up is we are on the corner," Gage replied in a hushed tone. "We're sitting there, waiting for you."

"Be there in five," Radar said.

He headed up to the house, and, just as he was about to cross the sidewalk in front, an explosion came, and the whole place blew up, sending him tumbling to the ground.

CHAPTER 6

SAMMY WAS OUT of the vehicle and raced to Radar, before anybody had a chance to stop her. She screamed at him, only to see him slowly gaining his feet again.

He grabbed her and pulled her off to the side. "Go back to the vehicle," he cried out.

"I can't. I won't leave you here."

"I'm coming. I'm coming."

She didn't know why he was so insistent on her going back. It's obvious the house was on fire, but, as he stumbled toward the car, he added, "They'll be here watching."

And, with a shock at his declaration, she bolted for the car and got into the back seat. He stumbled in beside her, as it took off. All manner of chaos was happening, as neighbors came out, sirens were too damn loud, and other emergency vehicles raced around. She groaned as she settled again in the vehicle, then turned and twisted at his side. "Are you okay?"

"I will be," he murmured. He reached up a hand to his face, and she winced.

"I'm not exactly sure what just happened, but you took a hell of a blow."

He nodded. "I did, but that's okay. I was just on the outside range of the blast."

"*Sure*," she muttered. "You need to see a doctor. That looks pretty rough."

"I'm sure it does, but it wasn't bad. We're all okay." He leaned toward Gage. "Did you see anybody?"

"No, the security vehicle, the ghost car that you tucked the guy into, is staying behind to see if anybody walks up."

"The only problem with that is, if they know that the snitch is in there, they'll put a bullet in his head."

Gage looked at him through the rearview mirror. "You want to warn Jonas about that?"

"I don't think he'll take that warning very well," Radar muttered.

"Nope, he sure won't."

"I don't care if he does or not," Sammy snapped. At Radar's side, she reached up a hand and pulled his hair away from his face. "What the hell were they doing? Anybody could have gotten hurt."

At that, Johnny just laughed from the front seat. "Remember? This is what bomb makers do."

"I know. I know. I know," she grumbled, as she scrubbed at her face. "I still don't like it."

"You're not supposed to like it," Gage noted. "That's why we do this. Remember?"

"Shit," she said. "I can't believe that asshole will get away with this again."

"Who said he's getting away with it?" Radar asked, looking at her.

She shrugged. "It seems he's getting away with it and ..." Then she stopped. "But hang on. ... That's not his MO."

"No, it's not, and that's another question. Was that a diversion, or was that a payback?"

"Payback," she declared instantly, frowning.

"Why would you say that?"

"Because he doesn't like having anybody's attention, and he doesn't like anybody tracking him. He doesn't like anybody interfering in his life," she explained, instinctively understanding this bomb-maker she'd been hunting for all these many months.

"Now you know why this had to happen, as far as he was concerned."

"Yeah, and yet it didn't," she muttered in disgust. "Was he really expecting everybody to be in there?"

"Yes, he probably was," Gage stated.

Sammy checked on Radar again, who was sitting back with his eyes closed. "He doesn't look good," she mentioned to anybody who would listen. "I think he needs to go to the hospital."

"I'm not going to any hospital," Radar argued in a mild tone.

She glared at him. "You don't have to be so macho all the time."

He laughed. "No, only when it counts."

"It doesn't count right now," she countered. "You can't just pretend to be strong, when you're obviously hurt."

"I'm not hurt, not in any way, shape, or form. I took a fall to the ground, but, other than that, I'm fine. It could have been a damn sight worse."

She groaned and sat back. "All the computers, all the stuff in the house …"

"What about it?"

"Everything is gone."

"Did you find out anything?"

"Maybe. I was just getting another address off a credit card. It was one I recognized."

At that, Johnny spoke up. "I recognized it too. It's back

at the homestead address."

She nodded.

"Which address is that?" Gage asked. She gave it to him, and he said, "Let's go check it out."

"What? Just like that, with no backup?" Sammy asked.

"We had backup," Radar noted in a mild tone. "I'm sure you saw what happened to it."

"Was anybody else hurt?" She gasped, then twisted to look behind them, which was ridiculous since they were long gone from the area. "I don't even know where we are," she said, turning back around and staring at the men. "When will this be over?"

"When we catch him," Gage declared. "Not until then."

"Dammit," she murmured, as she stared out the window. "There was something else on that second address I gave you guys. Something with the name. It was a version of the same name, but something was funny about it."

"Like what?" Johnny asked. "I didn't get a chance to even look at that."

She frowned, as she continued to think about it. "It was the same address, the same … as his daughter's birthday."

"Daughter?" Gage twisted in his seat to glance at her. "The bomb maker has family?"

"*Had* family," she corrected. "Because of his daughter's death. She died in Paris but they always spent time in London. Thus our focus on London and Paris."

"Oh, great, nothing worse than somebody who's got that kind of a revenge motivation behind them. Now I understand why he is so good at this. Guys like that, they don't care if they live or die. They just want to ensure that whoever was involved pays for it."

"I sure as hell didn't have anything to do with it, so I

don't know why I should pay."

"Because you're tracking him," Gage explained. "The minute you started that, you exposed yourself. Done deal."

She shrugged and settled back against her seat. "I'm not sorry."

"You aren't sorry yet?" Radar asked at her side. "However, if it gets any worse than this, you might very well be sorry. Do you have any family they can go after?"

She shook her head. "No, I don't, but Johnny does."

"His family already has security," Gage confirmed, "so I don't think that's an issue."

"You mean, the same security handling the very secure safe house," she said, with a smirk, a shocking reminder of what just happened.

"Not ours," Gage stated, "but, yeah, definitely the same idea."

"So obviously our next stop at one of the bomb maker's newest rentals is not very secure, is it?"

"Let's hope it's more secure than where we've come from."

"I want to go see this latest hidey-hole for Frenchie," Johnny said. "I don't trust him."

"I don't trust him either," Radar agreed, "but I'm not sure taking you there is a good idea because, if the bomb maker didn't know that we have this information, Frenchie surely will after that."

"Meaning we're being followed?" Johnny gasped.

"I would presume so, yes," Radar confirmed. "Anybody who's got satellite available to them could track us without any issue." He looked at Gage. "We need to get everybody else tracking vehicles from that scenario."

"Already on it," Gage noted. "I had them set it up when

we got the alert to get out of the house. Thanks for that, by the way."

"How did you know?" She turned and looked at Radar. "How did you know that was planned?"

"I didn't know if it was planned or not, but the young man I picked up outside that safe house had been doing the recon on the house and had the address in his pocket."

"But he was just looking to see if people lived there," she cried out in confusion. "It was just a matter of when we were found."

However, once that had been confirmed, it also meant an attack was guaranteed.

WHEN RADAR WALKED into the next safe house, he looked around, his instincts on full alert, but, even then, Sammy walked up behind him, as trusting as a lamb.

"Sit down in the kitchen, so I can clean up that head wound." When he frowned at her, she glared at him. "None of that macho crap. You can die from a simple infection, and you know it."

At that, Johnny snickered. "You better do what she says. When she gets like this, it's nearly impossible to do anything but." Johnny added, "I'll help Sammy find some medical supplies around here somewhere."

"Interesting," Gage noted, as he walked past Radar. "Bet your internal radar didn't pick up on that."

Radar glared at him, even though they were relatively alone for the moment. "What do you know about my own radar?"

Gage laughed. "Do you really think we work with just

anybody?"

"Sure, you do. You work with anybody as long as Levi or Bullard gives the okay," he muttered.

"That's true, but we'd already heard about your radar abilities."

"No, you didn't," Radar argued. "That's BS, since nobody knows anything about it."

"That's because you would like to think you're keeping it to yourself, but you should know better than that. Other people have skills too."

Radar eyed Gage, then asked him, "Speaking of skills, where's Riff?"

"I don't know. That's one for Terk. Riff is kind of his own man."

"Definitely something is different about him."

"There is, indeed, but I trust him."

"And you don't trust me?" Radar asked bluntly.

"I didn't say that," Gage replied. "However, I recognize Riff's power. It's obvious." Radar nodded at that, as Gage continued. "Riff does a terrible job of keeping it hidden. He's also very aware of his gifts, which is why it's easier to trust him, while, in your case, you're too busy denying them."

"It's not that I'm denying anything. Just not a whole lot of people in my world I can talk to about this stuff."

"That's why you need to spend some time with us. You probably think it's just your instincts."

"Isn't it?" Radar asked, with a flat tone. Then he looked around, clearly uncomfortable. "I also prefer privacy."

"We all do, but you still need some idea of what you're doing in order to increase it."

"Who said I wanted to increase it?"

"We all want to increase it," Gage admitted. "Don't be foolish. If there was a particular skill that you could develop, you'd do it in a heartbeat, wouldn't you?"

Radar studied him. "Sure, but how does one get into a school where you can develop this shit?" he asked in a mocking tone.

"That would be the school at Terk's place."

"School?" Radar repeated. He was stunned by Gage's response.

"It's more than a school. It's definitely a lifestyle. Terk took me on quite a few years ago, and I've been training with him ever since." Just then he was called away, and Radar looked over to see him talking with Jonas, who had just arrived.

Radar joined them and asked the status of the others. The conversation was intense, with low voices. He was allowed to mix into the conversation, but there were warning glances directed behind him. "Okay, so what's going on?"

"The one agent left behind with the snitch has been shot," Jonas shared in a harsh voice. "Both men are dead."

"Damn it," Radar snapped. "I would have never have left him alone if I thought they'd seen us. That I don't appreciate."

"No, I'm sure you don't. I'm not too happy about it myself."

"And they didn't catch anybody, right?"

"No, but …"

"I'm really hoping they caught it on satellite," Gage interrupted. "Give me a chance to go take a look." With that, he stepped out.

Turning to walk away, Jonas asked Radar, "Do you guys have your own satellite?"

"I don't know, but an agreement is in place with Levi."

"That makes sense because, Jesus, otherwise we're paying them too much."

"And if they don't have their own satellite, you're not paying them enough," Radar stated, with a hard look. "In this day and age, it's mandatory."

Jonas winced at that, "You're right. ... It is definitely mandatory, as these assholes likely have their own satellites."

"I think that's a given," Sammy interjected, as she walked up to Radar with first aid supplies. She pointed at a kitchen chair, and he sat, while she cleaned his head wound.

"What do you mean by that though?" Jonas asked Sammy.

"It's not so much that they have satellites but that they have access to other people's satellites. That makes it a lot easier. If whoever these people are you're talking about don't have satellite access, I would imagine they're doing the same thing."

"Maybe, but it's still not the same as having your own available."

"Sure, but not everybody can afford it."

"Maybe not, but, if anybody had tracked that one satellite, they should have gotten back to you by now."

At that, Gage rejoined them and handed over a piece of paper. "Two vehicles. Both black SUVs that look to be government vehicles approached the house within three minutes of the blast. They left after one man got out, presumably to put the incendiary device in place, and then left. By the time they had reached the end of the block, there was the explosion."

Jonas looked down at the piece of paper and shook his head. "But we don't have anyone identified, do we?"

"It's in progress, but those are the letters of the one set of license plates."

"Good enough." And, with that, Jonas headed off with his phone in his hand.

Gage turned to face Radar. "Are you okay?"

Radar nodded. "Yeah, but I decided to take Johnny's advice. It's easier to go along with this than argue." Radar pointed at Sammy and her medic skills.

Gage laughed at that and nodded. "I get it," he muttered. "Besides, it makes Sammy feel as if she's doing something normal and not so out of control, like everything else in her world right now."

As Radar thought about that, he agreed. "That's a really good way to look at it."

"It's got to be really hard on civilians who don't deal with this stuff all the time," Gage added.

"It must be brutal," Radar acknowledged, "but she seems to be holding up pretty well."

"*Hello*," Sammy said loudly. "I'm right here. You don't have to talk around me, and, better yet, you can talk to me."

"I thought we were," Gage added, with a smirk.

She glared at him. "Aren't you funny?"

"Yeah, I am. Sometimes anyway."

At that, Johnny walked over and smiled at her. "My family is doing okay. I just talked to them on the phone, and they're being moved to London."

"Where are they going?" she asked him curiously.

"For the moment they're heading to another safe house, but I think she'll probably head back to her family's place in Amsterdam."

"You're okay with that?" she questioned.

"I am," Johnny stated. "It's better that they go there

than anywhere else right now."

"What about government assistance?"

"They'll get her there," Johnny replied. "I think after that, the bomb maker and his associates are unlikely to chase us down that far."

Sammy shrugged. "I don't know. I didn't think they would chase us this far, did you?"

"*They* wanted to head in that direction, so what can I say," he muttered. "I would just as soon my family stay in lockup, but I'm not sure that is even something we can continuously utilize all this time."

"I suppose that's a point too. At the end of the day, somebody has to pay for all this."

"If you find the guys, then the cost is all a wash," Jonas stated, as he returned. "In the meantime, we need to get the bomb maker and his terrorist friends, and we need to get them fast. We just lost another agent, and he'd only been in the service for a year."

"I'm sorry," she said. "What about those rental addresses?"

He nodded. "We're on it, and this house is equipped with more computers for you guys."

She looked at him, packed up the first aid supplies she had used on Radar's forehead, then nodded. "I guess that's a hint, *huh*?"

"You're the ones who have tracked Frenchie this far every time. You give us an address, and something else blows up. I'm hoping that we can get to something ahead of time for once."

"He's after us again. I can tell you that much," she declared. "So why don't you just set a booby trap and accept that he'll be here within the next day?" With that suggestion left hanging in the air, she turned and headed out to find the computer room, with Johnny on her heels.

Jonas looked over at Gage. "Not a bad idea."

He nodded. "She's right. The bomb maker is very persistent. She might track him and his buddies, but we're still behind them every step of the way. Plus, while we're doing this, they'll be out making plans to set things in motion so they don't get stopped before it goes down."

Jonas nodded. "I didn't tell her, but we did find bomb-making equipment at the second address. The one that was a variation on his daughter's name, so that is huge. We've taken possession of it all."

"Which could have precipitated this attack too," Radar noted.

"I know, and, as much as I want to just lock down everybody and hide them away, we can't afford to. If Frenchie and friends have another bomb planted or they've accelerated their time line, we must have that information, and we must have it now."

Radar nodded. "I get it," he replied, in a mild tone of voice, "but you can't expect people to keep working without any rest, and they've been on the go for a long time. They'll both need a break."

At that, Jonas winced. "Not to mention the fact that they haven't had anywhere near enough food, have they?"

"No, they sure haven't," Radar agreed, "and we could use some too."

"Right back to that whole babysitting deal then. I'll get some plans in place. In the meantime, keep an eye on them and don't let anybody get close to the windows or go outside. Even moving food back and forth makes it suspicious as hell."

"If there's any food in the place, I can cook," Radar offered.

"Go check it out," Jonas stated. "If you can come up with something that would stop us from having to do a trip outside right now, that would be the best."

With that, Radar headed into the kitchen.

CHAPTER 7

SAMMY WORKED TIRELESSLY, not even sure at what point in time she'd started or even how long she'd been at it. When a warm hand landed on her shoulder, she jolted and looked up to see Radar standing there, a dimpled smile on his face.

He motioned over at Johnny, who was getting up. "Time for a food break, you two."

She stared at him for a moment, blinking owlishly, and then slowly nodded. "That's probably a good thing," she murmured.

"Yes, it is," Radar agreed. "Come on. It's in the kitchen."

She got up, stretched, and slowly walked to the kitchen, then looked over at Johnny. "I don't know about you, but it does feel as if we're getting somewhere."

"We're getting somewhere but just not fast enough," Johnny complained, giving her a tired smile. "Like you, I just want this over with."

"Yeah, but it's not that easy though, is it?" she murmured. "We do what we can, but there's no guarantee that any of this will be over with quickly." As they walked into the kitchen, she stopped and stared. "Good God, did somebody cook real food?"

"I did," Radar stated, looking over at her with a smile. "We didn't want to take the chance of ordering food in, of anybody seeing activity around the house."

She nodded in agreement. "No, I hear you," she replied. "We do have another location we're tracking down, and, on a whim, I've got several searches going. Hopefully something will pop while we eat."

At that, Jonas came in and asked, "What do you mean by several searches?"

"The bomb maker's a creature of habit," she murmured. "He's always using the same numbers, over and over again."

"Isn't that dangerous on his part?"

"It's very dangerous, and it's also something that most people would say is stupid, but, since the number always correlates to his daughter, who died, I guess it's the driving force behind him. He's doing what he's doing for her. So it might be something he's not even capable of changing. And, if that is the case, we also have to consider the fact that maybe Frenchie is planning an end game. Maybe he's tired of all this, or maybe whatever payback he's hoping for is this last job."

"Regardless," Jonas added, "we need to find him before he can do this again."

"Oh, I agree. You won't get any argument out of me on that." Sammy yawned. She sat down at the table and watched in amazement, as a large pot of spaghetti noodles landed at the center of the table, followed by a huge pot of sauce. "I am impressed that you can cook, and I, for one, am grateful that you did."

Johnny didn't even wait for anybody to say anything, serving himself. Then he looked over at her. She nodded and lifted her plate, and Johnny quickly filled it with spaghetti. Without any comment, he tucked into the food, eating as if he hadn't in weeks.

She stared at the food. It had been way too long since she'd had a healthy home-cooked meal. She was more than ready to enjoy this, and she smiled over at Radar. "So, a guardian who can cook, *huh?*"

At that, Gage chuckled. "It's almost like it's meant to be, isn't it?"

She frowned at him. "What does that mean?"

"The company I work with is called Guardian Security, or the Guardians for short," Gage shared.

She nodded, pointing at Radar. "I don't know whether he's part of your company or not, but he belongs there."

At that, Gage raised one eyebrow and looked over at Radar.

Radar shook his head. "Hardly the time or the place for that discussion," he muttered.

"I don't know," Gage said. "Levi says he doesn't have a ton of work for you just now."

"That's Levi's way of trying to keep me on a thread. He knows that I don't want to be locked down to a certain job, so he casts me about, with a job here and there. Never really tied down, never really without work."

At that, Gage laughed. "I would be willing to bet that Ice came up with that particular strategy. She has a way of getting a lot of people to do things they didn't think they wanted to do. But workload-wise, that sounds normal."

"Does it? It seems to me that way more problems are out there than I can really fix."

"There'll always be more out there than we can fix," Jonas noted, appearing at their side again. "Believe me. This isn't exactly where I thought I'd be spending my evening either."

She looked over at him. "And yet you're here."

"Of course I'm here," he replied. "As long as you guys keep pumping out information, I'm running this end of things, so we can track this down. However, believe me. I'll be ready for a few days off, when we're finally done here."

"Won't we all?" she muttered. She looked over at Radar. "Where will you go when you're done?"

He shrugged. "No clue. I haven't got that far yet."

"You should think about it," Johnny suggested, "because that day is coming." Such a positive note filled his voice that everybody relaxed.

"You're that confident you can track down this guy?" Jonas asked Johnny and Sammy.

"We have before," she declared, with a nonchalant shrug. "Which is why we ended up contacting you guys in the first place, but look how well that went." Jonas glared at her but didn't engage in the argument that she figured he thought she was after. "Listen. I'm not trying to pick a fight," she added gently, "but, from our perspective, we did everything right, and it still ended up wrong."

"It's not that you ended up *wrong*," Jonas clarified, "but this bomb-making guy either knew that you were doing it, or—"

Radar piped up. "It's the *or* that concerns me." He looked around at the table. "Is anybody else here but us?"

At that, Jonas replied, "It's just us. Andy is lying down."

"Right, so then the only other option—and not something I want to bring up—is whether you have a mole in your department."

At that, Jonas glared at him. "We already found one and sealed up that line of connection. But a second one? Yeah, that has been considered, but, so far, we haven't found any evidence of it."

"Interesting," Radar muttered.

"Why do you consider that the only other option?" Jonas asked.

"Because it's really all that makes sense. We all saw how soon they found the first safe house."

"If I didn't already have so much work to do, I would dig into that whole safe-house thing," she muttered, "because that pisses me off."

"I don't know about the guy lurking around and confirming we were there, but I highly doubt he deserved to die for it," Johnny noted.

"Neither did my agent, who was taking him back to central," Jonas snapped. "As far as I'm concerned, whoever killed them deserves a bullet himself."

"Oh, absolutely," Johnny agreed. "And that's what ends up giving us all this trouble. That whole *eye for an eye* thing, and, before you know it, there have been so many eyes taken that nobody can even remember what brought this on."

Sammy looked over at him. "We're almost done. You know that, right?"

"I know," he acknowledged. "Sometimes it is just not fast enough."

He continued to shovel in the food, while she watched and worried. He was usually the calm positive voice of reason, while her emotions were all over the place. Even a few minutes ago he'd been super positive. These mood shifts were unusual for him. She didn't like it. "Will you be okay?" she asked.

He nodded. "I'm always okay, whether I want to be or not. You know that."

"And ..." She did know that, but, at the same time, she couldn't help but worry about her friend. "I just know that this could go on a whole lot longer than we want, and you'll need to pace yourself."

He lifted his head and glared at her.

She shrugged. "I know you don't like it when I tell you that, but working ourselves to the bone and not taking this break won't help us. We have to be sensible."

"You be sensible," he stated, lifting his fork and pointing it in her direction. "I'll just work. I want my family back and for us all to have a life afterward again. No matter what you say, you don't have that same stress."

"No, I don't," she agreed, knowing that saying the wrong thing would set off the long-term friends into a fight, and she didn't have the energy to deal with that right now. "But that doesn't mean that I care to walk away from having a future myself," she muttered.

He didn't say anything to that, just continued to eat. When his plate was empty, he got up without a word and headed back to work.

She stared down at her plate. "I really want to stay here, but it feels very much as if I need to go too."

"And yet," Radar noted, eyeing her plate, "you didn't eat enough."

"I ate enough for now," she stated, with a smile. "If you want to keep my plate here, I'll come back in a bit and get some more. Right now, this is probably more than enough for my system. Not to mention all this stress is making me nauseated."

Giving the others a quick smile, she said, "I'll see you over at the computers, whenever you're done eating." She got up, grabbed a bottle of water from the fridge, then joined Johnny, who was already fully engaged and working away, completely focused.

"We will get him," she noted.

"We will," Johnny repeated, looking at her intently. "Sorry. I just can't sit and socialize when my whole world is hanging in the balance."

RADAR QUICKLY CLEANED up the kitchen, noting that the only person who stepped up to help was Gage.

"You getting any reading on this?" Gage asked.

"I think it's an inside job." Radar glanced around and added, "In fact, I don't see how it can't be."

Gage nodded. "Instincts telling you anything?"

"No. What about you?"

"Not necessarily," Gage said in a cagey voice, "but something is off."

"So, I understand from Levi that there's some extrasensory abilities within your team."

Gage's lips quirked, as he glanced at Radar. "That's one way to look at it."

"Is that true?"

"It is and it isn't. We can't do a lot of things, and there will always be some people we can't do anything with."

Radar frowned at that and then nodded. "It's like everything else, isn't it? Sometimes my instincts are right on, and sometimes they aren't. So, because they aren't always right on point, I have trouble always trusting them."

"And the minute you let your mind go there," Gage explained, "the trust is something you can't really expand on."

"Meaning?"

"You have to trust. You must learn to trust yourself, and then it develops more and more."

"What happens when it's wrong, especially when you need it to be right?"

"Then it's wrong, and what you do is look back at the warnings and the lessons you had to try and figure out just what it was you missed."

"Making a mistake in this line of work can cost lives."

"It absolutely can," Gage agreed, his tone serious. "Now I'm not saying it's easy, but, if you're interested in learning more and developing more, then Terk's is the place for you."

"You're seriously doing this Guardian Security stuff?"

"That's the formal name," he noted, with a half smile. "You might understand more if you ever get over to our place."

"Levi told me that, if I didn't like kids, I better avoid it."

At that, Gage looked at him. "Funny, I didn't get the feeling that you didn't like kids."

"I didn't say I *don't* like kids. It was just what Levi told me. Would you care to explain why he would say that?"

"Calum's the only one with kids yet," Gage explained, with a knowing look, "but a whole bunch of babies are coming very, very soon."

"What, you mean a couple of the women are pregnant?"

"Let's just say, *all* of the women are pregnant."

At that, Radar stopped and stared. "All of them? How many are *all?*"

He winced at that. "Everybody on the team has a partner, and they're all pregnant, eight women total," he said. "Turns out it's one of the side effects of this kind of energy."

At that, Radar whistled silently. "Did you guys all know that ahead of time?"

"We hadn't really considered it, since we were all single anyway. Then, all of a sudden, none of us were single, and it was way too late to do anything about it."

Radar started to laugh. "I'm sure that was a shock."

"Yeah, you could say that." Gage gave him a droll smile. "We'll have to tell you the whole story of that series of events, but we already knew about one pregnancy going into it, and very quickly the rest of us all ended up in the same position."

"Wow," Radar muttered. "I hate to say it, but there is such a thing as birth control."

"Yeah, now you tell me," Gage teased, with a chuckle, followed by a solemn nod. "Here's the deal. Birth control is great and is really effective, but apparently, in certain highly charged scenarios, it's useless."

"You're kidding? You guys were all using protection?"

"Yeah, of course we were, but I don't know what to say. Mother Nature prevailed."

Radar started to laugh. "I hope everybody is happy about it."

"Honestly the women are all thrilled."

"The women?" he asked, with a quirk of his eyebrow. "What about you?"

"I'm pretty thrilled myself," he admitted, with a deep chuckle. "I think it was just a bigger shock for some, more than others. And some of the relationships weren't nearly as long-term as we would have liked before this happened, but there's really no getting around it. Once it had already happened, we all got on board in a hurry, you know?"

"No," Radar admitted, still chuckling. "I can't imagine. I sure hope you guys have lots of help."

"We have an incredible amount of help and yet not nearly enough. And that's happening along with setting up the new business too. Levi gave me a bit of a rundown of the work you do, Radar, just not a ton of detail. I'm surprised he sent you."

"Or maybe he's decided that I should be with a partner," Radar suggested. "Levi's been on a big matchmaking kick for a while, and I'm wondering if that's why he sent me over to your group."

"We don't have anybody unmatched at the moment," Gage noted, "and honestly everybody found their partners more or less on missions."

"Yeah? That's what Levi told me too."

"Which would make Levi correct in this case, considering the job that you're doing."

"Maybe, but what does that have to do with coming to your place?"

"An interesting conundrum, isn't it? You've got somebody you really care about, but you're not sure where you'll end up with her."

He glared at him. "You don't know anything about that."

"I don't have to know because I see energy."

At that, Radar stopped. "What, like auras and shit?"

"Definitely the *shit* part," Gage confirmed, cracking a smile.

Just then they heard Jonas say something in a loud voice. They walked into the living room to see him glaring at Sammy.

"How the hell did you do that?" Jonas snapped.

"I don't have time for your shit, so I hacked into your satellite, and I'm using it to track Frenchie. If you don't like it, we'll talk about it when the job is over."

He turned and glared at Radar. "It's not supposed to be that easy."

At that, Radar turned and looked at Sammy and Johnny, who were both ignoring him.

"Apparently it *is* that easy," Radar noted. "I know that is a concern in terms of hacking in general. You attract somebody who wants to take down or to infiltrate a satellite that's supposed to be sending telecommunications all over the world. It's especially problematic if they do it with more than one satellite."

At that, Jonas nodded. "We can't have that shit happening." He glared at her. "If you can hack into it, does that mean you can also set it up so other people can't hack into it?"

She nodded. "Yeah, I sure could, but you don't pay me enough. Oh, wait. You're not paying me at all."

He groaned. "Everybody just wants money."

"No, everybody doesn't, but we do have rent to pay, food to buy, and I would like to think that, every once in a while, I might get a good cup of coffee," she replied in a waspish tone.

He sighed. "You're one of those people who needs coffee to work, aren't you?"

"No," she replied. "I'm one of those people who can't stand other people breathing down my neck." And she shot him a hard look. "So, feel free to back off."

He stepped back, muttering to himself all the while, then pulled out his phone, as if to make some complaint.

Gage pulled him aside. "You might not want to change the status quo until we're done here."

"She hacked into the satellites," he growled, "and I don't even know how many she can access."

"All of them," she snapped from behind him. "I already told you that we can talk about me locking them down afterward. I'm not doing it right now, and you don't want anybody else doing it right now either because it's giving us a bit of an edge. If Frenchie hasn't already utilized them himself ..."

"They're not supposed to be that easily accessible," Jonas repeated.

"They aren't," she confirmed, glaring at Jonas. "Do you think we're just some run-of-the-mill hackers?" Shaking her head at that, she returned to her work.

Radar found himself grinning like a madman, as he watched their interaction. He looked over at Gage. "Do you have people like Sammy over at Guardians?"

"We have two, and Sammy would fit right in," he declared, with a smile.

"Yeah, but do you need any more?"

"That's a whole different story."

At that, she looked over, then frowned and asked, "What? Are you trying to sign me up for a job or something?"

"Nope, not necessarily," Radar admitted cheerfully. "Unless the people who came to help you might need something."

"Oh, great, more blackmail," she said, rolling her eyes.

"I wasn't thinking about blackmail," Radar clarified. "Just keeping you doing what you're doing."

"Oh, I plan on it," she muttered. "I don't suppose there's more coffee, is there?"

"I'll go put on a fresh pot." With that, Radar headed back into the kitchen, still grinning. It was an interesting idea and provided a bit of a distraction from what Gage had said earlier about Radar's abilities. Radar found himself wondering whether it was possible to develop these instincts of his a little more.

Gage followed Radar into the kitchen.

Radar asked him, "How does that stuff work?"

Gage smiled. "I'll tell you what I know. It increases more when you are around people like us. It's as if all our abilities keep getting stronger, and, in some cases, we're getting more."

Radar frowned at that. "*More*, as in more abilities?" he asked, cautiously turning to look around. "Does Jonas know?"

"Jonas would call it woo-woo stuff and prefers not to think about it. I don't know about Andy, but I would presume he has no gifts and has no knowledge of our special gifts, and we should keep it that way."

"Thank heavens for that," Radar muttered. "I can't say I'd want to be part of anything that would make it public."

"Right, and see? That's the whole thing. It's all held pretty closely because ultimately it's about hidden weapons. It's all about making the most of what we have to do the job. If people find out that we can do the shit we do, it becomes a whole different ball game."

"Got it, and that makes good sense," Radar said. He put on the coffee, finished wiping down the kitchen, and said, "I'll go crash for a few hours, if you're all right with that."

"No, I think you should," Gage agreed. "Then we'll switch afterward. I'll take her the coffee." As Radar headed out of the room, Gage softly called out, "As you lay down, maybe send out a probe or two and see if anything sends your internal radar into a spin."

Radar stopped, turned, then frowned. "Probe?"

Gage smiled. "Think about it. Think about where your instincts are coming from and what they might be. Then see if you could increase them."

"Increase them?"

"Expand them, develop them, build on your feelings, something along that line," Gage explained. "Then, as you go off to sleep, send out whatever it is you think you would need to make that happen, and see what comes back."

Pondering that, Radar headed into the room in the back and laid down on the bed to give himself four hours of shut-eye. Then he would go see how Sammy was doing. He already acknowledged that it was all about her.

He didn't know how he'd become fascinated so quickly with her, but there was no doubt about it. The question was, how did she feel? Was anything there? A spark? Yes, he could see it, could feel it. But was she waiting to feed it more oxygen, to nurture it into a flame? Could they even do anything about it?

Things were such a mess right now that, as far as he was concerned, this was still a job, and absolutely nothing could be sorted out until they were on the other side of this op. Yet his mind kept tantalizing him about the possibilities. And the possibilities, if considered, were endless.

He was about to close his eyes and drop into a deep sleep when he remembered what Gage had said. Radar didn't know if it was possible or even just what Gage was talking about, but, taking it under advisement, Radar closed his eyes, sent out a probe.

Send back the details, if there's anything to be aware of.

With that, he drifted off to sleep.

CHAPTER 8

SAMMY STOOD, HER eyes barely able to even focus anymore, and she scrubbed her face, as she wandered around. She drank some more water and looked over at Johnny. He was a machine and hadn't taken a break yet. "Johnny, we need to take a break," she said.

He shook his head. "You go lie down for a bit, and, when you come back, I'll go."

She snorted at that. "What you mean is, I'll go sleep, then come back, and you won't go at all."

He looked over at her and shrugged. "We've got this to do. Are we getting any closer though?"

"That's the problem," she muttered, as she stared at her monitors. "I've got a whole pile of searches on the go right now, but I need some shut-eye."

He waved at her. "Go on. Don't waste time talking about it. Just grab the time and then come back."

With that, she nodded and headed to the bedroom that she had seen on the other side of the kitchen. She stopped and realized Radar was sleeping here. She stood in the middle at the doorway and watched him. Gage came up behind her and mentioned, "Another bed is in there, if you want to crash."

"I don't want to disturb him," she whispered. "He needs sleep too."

"He needs it a whole lot less than you do, and there are two beds. So it's not as if you'll disturb him."

She asked, "Is there another bedroom?"

"There is, but Andy is lying down, and so is Jonas."

"Oh, right. Fine then. Radar's room it is." She shrugged, then headed to the small bed on the other side of him. She curled up but there were no blankets. It was just a mattress with a fitted sheet, but, as she struggled to get comfortable, Gage came back in again with a blanket.

She smiled as he tossed it over her. "Thanks," she muttered and slowly closed her eyes. She would have stayed asleep except that she heard something, a noise beside her, which had her looking around. There was Radar, prone in the bed but seemingly frozen in place, muttering, constantly muttering. She snuck out of the room and went to get Gage. She asked him, pointing back to the room, "Is Radar okay?"

He looked at her and bolted to his feet. They both stepped into the bedroom to see Radar still lying flat on the bed, not moving, still muttering to himself. Gage tilted his head, as if listening to Radar. "Yeah, he's fine."

She frowned at him and asked, "How is that fine? Is that nightmares? Is this what happens to you guys when you do these missions?"

"In this case it's a whole lot different," Gage shared. "Maybe you should go rest in the other room. You won't get any sleep, not with him like that."

Just then Radar's eyes opened, and he stared at them both. An odd expression covered his face, as he looked at Gage. Then Radar glanced at her, eyed the bed beside his, and ordered, "Come on and lie down."

"That's what I was doing, but then you started muttering in your sleep."

His eyebrows shot up. He looked over at Gage. "Was I?"

Gage nodded. "Yeah, but it's okay."

At that, he nodded. "I've had all the sleep I need anyway. I'll get up, so you can both get a nap." Hopping up, he walked into the small bathroom.

When he came out a few minutes later, Sammy decided it was probably the best opportunity she would get for a nap, so she went back to stretch out.

Gage walked over to the bed that Radar had just vacated and crashed down beside her. She watched as Radar headed out of the room. One part of her wanted to follow him and to ensure he was okay. Another part wanted to ask Gage a million questions as to why he was okay with whatever *that* had been, but she could see from the surprise on Gage's face that he'd been shocked about something, yet had come to terms with it very quickly—which was something else she didn't quite understand.

The good thing was that Gage wasn't concerned. It was all good, or at least she felt it was. She closed her eyes and drifted off to sleep.

She wasn't even sure what woke her next, but she woke up with a start and instantly sat up. She was alone in the room. She checked her phone and saw that she had been asleep for about four hours. She stumbled to the bathroom, washed her face, used the facilities, and then headed out to the room where the others were, deep in some discussion. "What happened?" she asked.

Gage looked up at her and smiled. "We might have caught a break."

"A break would be nice," she muttered, as she yawned and collapsed beside Radar on a nearby couch. "What's going on?"

Gage smiled. "Besides the fact that we think the rental house is about to come under attack," he stated, so calmly that it didn't even hit her for a moment, "it seems Johnny has found the phone number for this bomb maker, and we're tracking him live."

She stared at Gage, looked over at Johnny, shocked. He was weary to the bone and clearly exhausted, yet smiled.

"Yeah, the numbers you ran were right, and I tracked the phone calls, and it seems to be Frenchie."

"Wow," she muttered. "So much happened while I was asleep."

"I told you it would. I set some things in motion, thinking, when you got up, we could figure out a plan from there, and that's where we're at."

"Was anybody even going to wake me?" she asked in an accusing voice.

"I would," Radar stated, "but I also knew you needed the sleep."

She shrugged. "What about the other guys?"

"We haven't woken either of them yet," Gage replied.

"Any particular reason?"

"Yeah, decisions."

She raised an eyebrow. At that, Radar leaned in closer, wrapped his arms around her to give her a hug, then whispered against her ear, "We think there's a mole."

She looked up at him and then nodded. "Yeah, I was thinking the same thing, but I hadn't found any proof."

"That's what we need you to look for now."

"On it," she said. "You make the coffee, and I'll head back in that direction." She sat down at her computer and found some of her searches had come up with results. She studied them for a moment, and a fat smile broke on her face. When the coffee came, she looked over at Radar and whispered, "Bingo."

He frowned at her.

She nodded. "Better get Gage." When he came walking in beside Radar, she pointed out the numbers that had been accessed. "Recognize any of these?"

He shook his head. "No, I don't. Should I?"

"Maybe not," she said, "but you might want to check with Jonas."

"So, you don't think Jonas is part of it?"

"No, I don't," she stated, "but somebody he's working with at the office definitely is."

At that, Jonas stumbled toward them, rubbing his face. "What did I just hear?"

She frowned and asked, "How secure is your office?"

"I always say it's secure," he replied, "but we've certainly had moles in the past."

"You've got another one now too."

"Can you prove it?"

She nodded. "Pull out your phone and tell me if this number is in your contacts." She read it off.

He nodded. "It is. Why?"

"Because it's also a number that we think the bomb maker has connected to directly."

He looked at her and swore. "Seriously?"

"Yeah. Seriously."

"You've got the number for the bomb maker now?"

"It's one of the searches that I left with Johnny, while I headed in to crash," she explained. "I was pretty sure I'd found it, but we had to connect a lot of the other people to it, and now we're tracking it. As you can see"—she pointed to another monitor—"that's where it is at this point. Now, it's heading into downtown Paris."

"Well, shit, how do we know he's not about to set up an attack?" Jonas asked her.

Johnny walked in just then and replied, "I think he is." He held up his phone, and there was a text message. He looked over at her. "I contacted one of the men I've worked with several times to keep an eye out if this number was beeped and whether any of these names triggered something. We can't watch everything all the time, so I asked him to help, and he just notified me that this vehicle passed one of the checkpoints."

"What vehicle?" Jonas asked, suddenly all business.

Johnny gave him the license plate number. "It's a small white service truck, like for internet and telephone companies. There's a good chance a bomb is in it."

RADAR STUDIED THE satellite image in front of him. "But there's three of them." He pointed out the trio of similar vans. Using as much technology as they could, they still only grabbed two letters off one of the vans. Radar looked over at Jonas. "I'll go after them," he said.

Jonas frowned. "But we have my guys for this, right?"

At that, Radar hesitated because, of course, that wasn't his job here. Just because Radar wanted to run about and take care of things didn't mean that he was the one to do it. He glanced over at Sammy, who was still working away on the computer. Yet he could see the fatigue pulling at her, the stress tensing her shoulders, her back hunched over. Radar asked Jonas, "Do you have any best guess as to which one of these is our perpetrator?"

Without missing a beat, Sammy answered, "Personally I would say all three."

Radar smiled. "That would be my guess as well." He looked at Jonas. "How many men have you got on this?"

"As many as I need," he snapped, as he walked away, talking into his phone.

She looked up at Radar. "Do you really think you can do anything?"

"That's the thing, … just because we might track these three trucks, that doesn't mean that they aren't tracking us as well."

"Do you mean that Jonas's team isn't or that these guys aren't tracking their own progress?" she asked.

"I suspect they're tracking their own progress," Radar said, "because, if you think about it, it would be easier for them to sort out whether they have a tail on them or not."

She nodded. "If they have three of these vans, what's to stop them from having others?"

"Can you run down any of them from the rental addresses?"

With a surprised look, she quickly opened up new window and started cross-matching. "No, not from those latest addresses," she stated. "However, there is a link from another apartment in that same building."

He looked at her. "That's a little too obvious, isn't it?"

She frowned at that. "But it keeps everything nice and close."

"I suppose," he hesitated, "and does it come up with any peculiar activity?"

She brought up the van and added, "We'll have to search for it. I don't have any way to track it down—unless it's a rental too," she said suddenly. Then she quickly went into the databases on the rentals. "It's not a rental, but it was at one time," she shared.

"See if it's got any GPS tracking on it."

She headed back into the websites.

At this point, even Johnny came over to take a look. "I need to sleep, but if something is breaking—"

"I don't know that something is breaking, so much as there might be a fourth vehicle."

"Frenchie won't stop at three, not if he thinks four would do the job," Johnny noted. "Everything about this is important to him."

"Do we know any particular reason for a suspected location?" Radar asked them.

At that, Johnny looked at him. "Oh shit." He quickly walked over to his computer and started punching keys. Almost as if something had struck a chord, he turned back and said, "He and his daughter used to go to a series of cafés a lot, before she was killed at one of them."

Radar frowned at him. "How was she killed?"

"Shot accidentally by the police," Johnny admitted. "They were after an armed suspect, running in and out of storefronts. She and her father, our bomb maker, were in the restaurant at the time. Just as they came out onto the street, the shooting started, and they were caught in the crossfire. She took a bullet and went down."

"Frenchie blamed the police?" Radar asked him.

"In this case it was a police bullet, but it wasn't their fault. They were trying to get the shooter inside."

"So, it was a case of being at the wrong place, at the wrong time, and, for that, Frenchie's determined to make the world pay."

"He had the time and the means, and this was just the

trigger," Gage explained. "We've seen that happen more than enough times."

Radar had to acknowledge that point too. "Okay, so we have a location, and we have four possible vehicles."

When Jonas stepped back in a moment later, he handed Gage a sheet of paper and said, "Four vehicles. This is the location that they are most likely to attack."

Gage reviewed it and asked, "Why there? I don't know if that'll be a big-enough opportunity for him."

"Maybe not, but, if we consider the fact that his daughter was killed there and that some big rally is scheduled in that area today, it suddenly looks bigger."

Gage looked at it again and nodded. "Godammit, yes. A big political rally is probably en route right now," he noted and jumped on his phone again. He looked down at Johnny and Sammy. "We still don't have a face."

"I have a partial face," Sammy shared, "but all the IDs seemed to suggest a chameleon."

"It's not hard to change your appearance in our world these days," Gage added, as he stepped forward to look at the image that she showed him. "That's not enough for anybody to recognize. It'll be more his whole body that we'll end up catching him on."

Jonas returned moments later. "I'm leaving," he stated abruptly. "I have to go handle this. I'm meeting with French authorities on the way. It's going to take all of us to mobilize a massive effort to clear the area. We're already out of time."

"As soon as you do that," Johnny noted, "Frenchie will abort."

"Yes." Jonas nodded. "We have no choice. We can't take the chance of all these people dying just because it's where his daughter was killed. My sympathies to him. Believe me.

Yet we can't let all those people be sitting ducks."

"It also doesn't make a whole lot of sense really," Sammy suggested. "I get that's where his daughter was killed, but, to me, that would be more of a secondary target."

At that, everybody froze. Jonas slowly turned toward her and asked, "What? You know I really don't want to hear that, right?"

She looked over at Johnny. "What do you think?"

"I don't know," he began, "but you're right. Generally his targets are big, … like *big*, big."

"There's a rally," Jonas cried out in frustration. "How much bigger does he want? There'll be thousands of people there."

"Yes, thousands of people," she agreed, "but it's also too impersonal in a way."

"Impersonal?" he asked, staring at her in shock. "Frenchie sets off bombs. That's inherently impersonal. It's very hands off, and he could be miles away before they blow. What's more impersonal than that?"

"That's the problem," she noted. "That's why it feels off."

"I don't want to hear *off*," Jonas snapped. "If you've got anything to give us, then give it to us. Otherwise text me," he snapped, walking to the front door. "I'm on my way downtown to deal with this."

"You're putting yourself in the line of fire," Gage reminded him.

"I don't have any choice," Jonas said. "Tactical forces will be down there, and God knows how many cops. I can't even begin to think about trying to clear those streets. Yet we must make it happen now. If you've got anything to offer, then contact me. Otherwise assume I'll be incredibly busy for the next few hours." He stopped at the doorway, gave them a hard look, and added, "If you're wrong …"

"We know," Radar noted, "but it's not their fault if they are."

Jonas nodded. "No, it's not. And, hey, you never know. I might see you again." And, with that, he was gone.

His words caused Sammy to gasp, while she scrubbed the fear and the stress from her face once again. "God, this is just so intense."

"It's crazy intense," Gage agreed. "However, if we can't do anything else or can't collect more information, we're at a sit-and-wait stage."

"I never do those very well," Radar admitted, as he studied the satellite images. "When you mentioned a secondary target, what did you mean?"

"In any communication we've ever found, Frenchie has always held the police officer who fired the bullet that killed his daughter personally responsible."

"Did you tell Jonas that?"

She looked over at Johnny, who nodded. "We did early on, but I don't think that cop is even in the service anymore."

"That doesn't mean Frenchie won't do something about it," Radar noted. "Do you have address for this guy?" It took a little longer than he would have liked, but, when it came up and wasn't far away, he nodded. "You guys are fine here, right? Maybe I'll go take a drive."

Gage looked at him and frowned.

"I know, not smart, but, at the same time, that cop's right close by. If the bomb maker holds one person responsible, then it would be this cop."

"So, you'll go after the bomb maker on your own?" she

asked Radar.

"Not what I want to do, but—"

"Let me come with you," she offered.

Radar shook his head. "Hell no, you're safe here. Stay behind and see if there's any other information you can find."

"You don't even know what he looks like," she said.

"And you do?" Radar asked.

She hesitated, looked back at Johnny, and then admitted, "Yeah, I've met him a couple times."

"What?" Radar and Gage both roared in shock.

She winced, and Johnny explained. "When we were first starting out tracking him, we weren't sure exactly who we were tracking. So, yeah, we tried a few other methods of following him. In a nutshell, here is how it went. She contacted him and tried to use that as a way to get near enough so we could get some tracking on him. She was able to track him to a coffee shop."

Radar and Gage frowned at them, looking back and forth between her and Johnny.

Johnny continued. "He wasn't in there very long, and, when he saw her, there was almost a note of recognition that she was trouble because he bolted, but she's the one who saw him," Johnny explained reluctantly. "That's all."

"*That's all?* Why has no one ever told Jonas that?"

"We figured it was safer if nobody knew."

"Yeah, it is safer if nobody knows, as long as the damn bomb maker doesn't know," Gage snapped. "So, if the bomb maker knows that Sammy is after him, then that's a big problem, especially if the bomb maker's cleaning up or checking out. In which case, he'll ensure that you're not around to talk. That's a huge problem."

"And that is a problem," she confirmed. "So let me come along."

"What good will that do?" Radar stared at her. "Except for giving me somebody I have to look after, which I really don't want to do."

She glared at him. "Maybe not, but I also know who his partner is."

"What?" he snapped, staring at her. "How much of all this have you guys been dealing with?"

She shrugged. "We've been looking into this for a long time. We gave all the information to Paris authorities. We figured it's how we ended up on Interpol. We did try to tell MI6, but honestly I don't know how much they even looked at it or acted on it."

At that, Johnny added, "It goes back to the fact that we think there's a mole in the department."

"Do you have any idea who?" Gage asked.

"No, but Jonas does. We gave him a number, and it was in his contacts."

"Just take her with you and keep her safe, while you do a quick check to make sure that the officer is okay," Johnny suggested to Radar.

"We could just phone him," Gage offered.

At that, she looked up the number and handed it to him. "You could," she stated. "He won't know me from Adam."

He gave her a hard look, as he stepped away from the group for a bit. When he came back, he shook his head. "No answer."

"No, and that doesn't mean anything except that he could be asleep," Sammy noted. "By the way, I speak French." She looked over at Radar. "Do you?"

He glared at her. "I make do."

"Yeah? Well, I make do a lot faster."

"It's dangerous," he muttered, shaking his head.

"I've been in this since the beginning, and I would really like to see it come to an end." With that, she got up and walked across the room. "Come on. We're wasting time."

CHAPTER 9

A POWERFUL HELICOPTER made short work of the trip to Paris. Now in a black car racing through traffic, Radar finally voiced his worry. "You know this is a bad idea, right?"

"Possibly, yes," she agreed. "But, since I started this, I need to finish this. Afterward maybe I can leave Paris and the hunting of bad guys for good and have a life."

"Yet it wasn't your family destroyed."

"No, but I also committed to help Johnny, and I can't let that one go." Radar didn't say anything, and she looked over at him curiously. "Why do you do what you do?"

He smiled. "I don't know. I've always felt the need to do this. I'm just not used to interacting with civilians who have that same need."

"But see? We don't feel like civilians at this point. The bottom line is that I started it, and so I must finish it. Plus I need to make sure that Johnny can get out with his family."

"His family was picked up, and they are safe," he reminded her.

"None of us are safe," Sammy replied, "as we have seen here, time and time again. Plus I also think we have more work to do with Jonas, which I think would be a bigger problem."

"I wish you would stay at the safe house and work on

that part," he muttered.

"Johnny is better at that sort of thing. He's better off focused on that instead of what we're doing."

"Why is that?"

She shrugged. "Anything to do with this bomb maker guy gets Johnny quite irate. His uncle was killed, but Johnny was there at the time, or close by, at least. Not being able to do anything and not having any awareness or warning of what was going on has plagued him ever since. I want him to be free of this."

"How do you two know each other?" he asked.

"University," she stated. "We never went out together in that sense, but we were friends nonetheless, really close friends. Over the years that just developed more and more. I was there when he met his wife. I was there when they got married. I was there for the birth of his first child," she shared. "Most people say that men and women can't have platonic relationships, but they're wrong. It's been one of the best relationships in my life."

Radar smiled at that.

"Johnny's forever telling me to go find my own partner and to forget about him."

Startled, Radar frowned at her.

"No, I don't think of him romantically at all, but, because I haven't found a partner, he's afraid that we're too close. He thinks I would be better off if we weren't this close, so I should make a point of going out and meeting people."

"When you're on a mission like this, it's hard to meet people. You can't tell them what you're doing. You can't explain the drive to do it, so you end up alone."

"Exactly," she murmured. "And that's what's happened. Plus you can see how close to death we've come a couple times," she added. "I want a future. I want this to be over, so I can turn around and move forward."

"I sure don't have a problem with that. A future is what you should have."

"Maybe, but that means putting away this bomb maker first," she declared.

"Do you really think he'll get put away?"

Startled, she glanced at him. "You think he'll die?"

"You tell me. You know as much about him as anybody else. You've tracked him, so you must have a pretty good idea of who he is at this point."

She pondered that. "No, I think you're right. I think there was a designated end point for him, but I don't know what brought it to this …"

"Did you ever check any medical records for Frenchie?" Radar asked her curiously.

She gasped. "I never did."

"You've got a laptop with you." Radar pointed it out on the seat between them.

She snatched it up and started working.

"If you have internet."

She laughed. "Yeah, not a problem." And, with that, she continued to work and then whistled silently. "That's interesting, and it explains this whole scenario too."

"What's that?" he asked.

"Frenchie has cancer. He's dying."

"Do have a time frame?"

"According to his medical records, he has dragged it well past that."

"Ah, so this is his end game," Radar noted. "He'd rather go out this way than leave it to whatever cancer that's destroying his body."

She stared at the screen in front of her. "He tried various treatments, but nothing worked, and there's a DNR on file here. If he goes down, he's not to be resuscitated."

"And yet he's mobile?"

She frowned at that. "I would have to do some more research on what this cancer does, but chances are, he is mobile but showing his age."

"Maybe showing his mental decline too?" he asked, looking over at her.

"No way to know that there is any mental decline," she replied. "Why?"

"Just the consistent use of his daughter's numbers. Her birthdate, age, etc."

"I think that's all more symbolic than anything," she suggested.

He nodded. "That's possible, I guess. Not that it makes much difference to us right now. What's important to understand is that this is it for him. He won't be taken in, and, if this final bomb event brings him to a faster end than the painful cancer one he's heading for, the one he's already going through right now, I think he'd be okay with that."

"Are we thinking suicide bombing?" she asked.

"We can't rule it out. Yet, at the same time, I don't think that would necessarily be his choice, but who knows."

At the beep of her phone, she said, "I just got a message from Johnny. Jonas has a full team set up, and they're busy clearing out that plaza."

"That's good," Radar replied. Yet she frowned and didn't say anything. "It's not good?" he asked. "You don't seem terribly pleased."

"It's good, and yet it's not," she explained. "It's great if all those people got a chance to escape, but it's not so good if it means Frenchie will abort that location or will use it as a decoy to get all the police into one place."

"I wondered about that too," Radar confirmed. "I did mention it to Jonas, but he told me that their choices were limited."

"It's always down to logistics, manpower, timing, data," she stated. "That's why these bombers do this, right? It's always a bait and switch." She was lost in her thoughts, just blabbering now.

"So, what's the second location?" he asked her.

She frowned. "The second location was my first location of choice, but Johnny didn't agree."

"What was it?" he asked, glancing at her.

"Not too far from that same plaza was his daughter's most favorite place. He used to take her there all the time."

"So you don't think he would go to the location where she was killed?"

"Depends on whether it's a memorial," she suggested. "If it is, wouldn't you want to do it there? A place where she loved to go. A memorial instead of a place of hate, where she was killed," she murmured.

He looked at her for a moment, then quickly changed lanes, as he moved the vehicle in the direction they now needed to go. "That's what this is all about, isn't it? It's his motivation for this chaos. If we can figure that out, we've got him."

"Considering he's dying, I don't know if he's still full of revenge and hate anymore. Maybe he's realizing that he'll be joining his daughter soon. In his mind, he is sound, and maybe he's planning something there to honor her somehow."

"How do we figure it out?"

She shrugged. "I don't know. I really don't know what to say to that."

He pondered that. "Have you ever been to this location where she loved to be?"

"No, it's an outdoor gym park," she noted. "His daughter was really big on gymnastics."

"You want to punch it into the GPS? Let's see how far away it is," he said.

"Instead of going directly to the cop's place, and I want to hit there too, but we could very easily be running out of time. So let's check out this park first."

"If everybody is not at the right location, chances are that's exactly what we're doing—running out of time."

While she tinkered with the GPS, Radar phoned Gage. "I don't know what special skills or talents anybody on your team has, but we could use them. Sammy suggested another potential location for this to go down."

"Why another location?" he asked. "I thought we had the bomb site locked down."

"Not according to something she just brought up." Radar quickly explained how Frenchie has cancer, how this is his end game, how it's a memorial for his daughter.

"Oh, that's interesting, and motivation is everything."

"So, how do we find out more?"

"I don't know, but what if it's something that's fluid?" Gage asked him.

"Meaning?"

"I'm just guessing here, but what if they would do the one but had a backup location if they ended up having to abort?"

"But then the motivation is very confused."

"Yeah," Gage agreed, "and he's also dying, so how much

of this is just a need to complete the job before he is incapable of physically doing it?"

"That's another ugly point too," Radar noted.

Gage groaned. "Look. I might have a way to get some information, so hold tight. So now I presume you won't check on the cop first but are heading toward this second location or to Johnny's first choice?"

"If there's no activity around the first place, and you guys have all the vehicles on the go, I'm heading to this new location, the second place."

"Is that what your instincts are telling you to do?" Gage asked curiously.

Radar wasn't exactly sure why Gage was asking, but Radar responded with certainty, "Yes, that's a strong one. So, yes."

"In that case, that's where you go," Gage replied easily. "When it comes to instincts, we never fool around."

Radar smiled at that. "Thanks. I figured you would say the opposite to that."

"Oh, hell no," Gage corrected. "Believe me. Everybody on our team has been there. When our instincts are screaming, … you listen. That's the only way that they develop too."

"I don't know about developing, but honestly, while we were in the first safe house, they were screaming pretty heavily. Matter of fact I just assumed it was good intel, so I was with you guys leaving that location. Right now, I'll follow my—Wait. … Hold on. … Get the hell out, Gage."

"As in *right now*, right now?"

"Get the hell out of that house," he roared into the phone, as he pulled off to the side of the road to look at her. "I don't know if you have a way to contact Johnny, but tell him to get the hell out of that house."

Startled, she grabbed her phone. When Johnny answered, he was out of breath. "Are you getting out?" she asked.

"Yeah, I don't know why. Something just happened, and we got orders to run. Call you back."

"I don't know what happened," she told Radar, "but Johnny's on the run."

"Good." Radar sighed. "That's what we need."

"If you say so. It affirms the fact that we're not safe at all. Whether in two different safe houses or even in MI6 offices, we won't be safe until that son of bitch is behind bars."

"Our guys are out of there now, so they should be good to go."

"You think so?"

"Yes, and I think it goes back to the damn mole."

"In that case my vote is Andy," Sammy declared.

He startled, as he stared at her in shock. "Why Andy?"

"Because he's been there with us from the beginning. The HQ of MI6, then the first safe house, and now this second one. He was also part of the team since the beginning of this investigation." She pondered all that for a few moments and shrugged. "My instincts say Andy."

"But you don't have anything to back it up?"

"Nope, I sure don't."

He quickly sent Gage a text, warning him what she said about Andy, then reminded Gage too that there was absolutely no proof to back it up. He got a thumbs-up and a reply text, confirming they were on the move. But Andy got Gage's vote too. Which was about as good as Radar could get right now. "I don't know where they're going, but they're definitely moving," Radar shared with Sammy.

"Good. Can we move now too?"

He pulled back into the traffic. "It would have been helpful if you'd mentioned something about Andy earlier."

"It doesn't do me any good to throw somebody under the bus like that, especially if I don't have any proof. It's still just an idea and needs a critical look at the facts."

"No, but it would have given us something to go on."

"It just would have stirred up bad feelings from Jonas, since it's one of his guys."

"You don't think he's considered Andy already?" he asked her curiously.

"I thought Andy got mentioned before, and Jonas said Andy had already been cleared."

"I think you're right on that, but just in case ..." He pulled out his phone and driving carefully, quickly sent Jonas a text. "There. It's taken care of."

She looked at him and asked, "Are you warning him?"

"Just suggesting that Jonas take another look at his guys," Radar explained. "I'm not throwing Andy under the bus, but I want to make sure that nobody has a chance to get Johnny and his family because of insider information."

"What about telling Gage? You don't seem to be too bothered about warning him."

Radar contemplated it for a moment and nodded. "I'm not. Not at all. As far as I can see, he's perfectly capable of taking care of whatever comes his way."

She smiled. "Now that makes him a good team member."

"Exactly," he agreed.

"Besides, there's something weird about him."

"Weird?"

"Yeah, *weird*-weird," she clarified, "like woo-woo weird."

He stared at her in shock. "What do you mean, woo-woo weird?"

She laughed. "Just like you and your internal radar."

"Whoa. That's *instincts*."

"Whoa. That's *radar*," she stated in a mock imitation of him.

He glared at her. "I don't have any woo-woo stuff in my world."

"Yeah, of course you don't," she said, with an eye roll.

"Do you?" he asked cautiously, looking at her.

"As if I would tell you, when you're obviously so anti–woo-woo stuff."

"I'm not against woo-woo stuff," he protested, as he drove, furiously following the GPS directions. "Still, that's a hell of a thing to spring on a guy."

"No, it's not," she scoffed. "If you were any more in tune, you would have already figured it out."

"Figured what out?" he asked, glaring at her. "Where the hell has *this* Sammy person come from? Up until now you've been really meek and mild."

"Yeah, well, I *was* meek and mild, but now I've got my chutzpah back again," she claimed, and then she cut loose with a boisterous laugh. "Which is really bizarre, considering our circumstances."

"Yeah, I could certainly agree with that."

"Whatever," she muttered, "but you need to understand that your radar is more than just instincts."

"How do you know?" he asked, glancing at her.

"Because I have some skills of my own," she answered coyly. "What do you think makes me so good on computers? I hunt, but I'm a cyberhunter, not exactly something anybody in the woo-woo world has heard of."

He stared at her, blinked several times, returned to his driving, then finally asked, "Are you serious?"

"Yeah, I'm serious," she responded. "I'd hoped that you might be a little more open, considering you do it yourself. Gage is certainly open."

"Gage?" He eyed her suspiciously.

"Yeah, but then he's already a die-hard woo-woo afficionado."

Radar snorted at that. "Do you just make up this shit on the spur of the moment or what?"

Again she laughed. "Nope, not necessarily, but, if you didn't see it before, I'm not about to tell you now."

"Well, you just did," he stated in frustration. "And I don't like it."

"No, and that's why you're still stuck on your *instincts* thing. Why do you think Gage is always asking you about your instincts?"

"Because he trusts instincts."

"Yeah, because he also knows it's more than that," she added, with a headshake. "Whatever. ... Forget I even mentioned anything," she muttered.

"How am I supposed to do that?" he asked, shaking his head. "It's not exactly a conversation you forget."

"Which is why I don't bring it up with anybody, but I thought that maybe you might be different. However, I was wrong."

He quickly changed lanes at the urging of the GPS directions, and Sammy said, "You're almost there."

"What exactly do you do with your woo-woo stuff?"

"Computer work. And, no, before you ask what you're about to ask, I'm not a hacker. I'm a data analyst. I basically do computer work to hunt and to find things. I've never really done much fieldwork."

"Any government connection?"

"Nope, really not a big fan of government. Too many rules and regs for my liking."

At that, Radar burst out laughing. "Now that makes sense to me."

She flashed him a grin. "I think you're out here on some test too."

"What do you mean, a test?" he asked, looking at her in astonishment. "I'm here because Levi offered my services to Terk."

"Terk? Do I know that name?" She pondered it. "Oh, *Terk*." She looked at Radar in delight. "Are you with him? Is that who Gage works for? Oh, wow, this is even better than I thought."

"Whoa, whoa, whoa. What in the hell are you talking about?"

She stared at him and sighed. "Oh, shit, you really don't know, do you?"

"No, I really don't know, and you're starting to piss me off," he admitted, sounding aggrieved.

She smirked. "That's just because it's going on all around you, and you really weren't aware"—she shook her head in wonder—"which just goes to show how blinding your blinkers are."

"Yeah? Okay, so stop with the insults and increase the explanations."

She sighed. "Terk is a fairly well-known subject to me. I don't want to use the term *psychic*, but maybe psychic is the right word for him. When I first heard about him, he was part of a top-secret government agency that was doing remote viewing. Now that is an oversimplified explanation of the work they did, but they went way past that. Then I heard his team was abruptly disbanded. I'm not sure what happened, but, according to what I'm hearing now, maybe they've gone private. I really should contact them and see if they need anybody."

He just frowned at her.

"So, is he the one you're working for?" she asked.

"Yes, he is," he replied reluctantly, "but I don't know anything about all those other things you just brought up."

"However, you do know it's true. You're just not really ready to say anything about it." He glared at her, and she smiled impudently. "See? I can even tell from the look on your face that you know what I'm talking about, but you're just surprised that I know anything."

"Yeah, I am surprised that you know anything about that. It was pretty top secret."

"Yeah, but I tripped over him on the internet. And, while the net is a massive place, in other ways, it's really quite small."

"No, it's really not a small place at all, and I don't think Terk would be terribly happy that you tripped over him."

She shrugged. "All kinds of chaos goes on in the world, all at the same time, and Terk seemed to have been a major part in it. So, when I tripped over him, it just made sense to check up and to see how things were going. However, as far as I could tell, everything was going well." She was thrilled to hear Radar was working with Terk, and it made so much sense now.

"Jesus," Radar muttered.

"It's not all that different than the internal radar for you," she noted, "so just deal with it."

"*Deal with it*, she says, like that's an easy thing."

"You already know that your skills are beyond normal instincts."

"I just have really good instincts," he reiterated, like a broken record.

She smirked at him. "Yeah, you sure do." And then she fell silent, looking ahead. "Up here." She pointed.

He followed her instructions, and they came around to a parking lot. On the other side was a vast field with outdoor gym equipment, a playground, plus malls and stalls. It was massive, and something that he'd never really seen before. "Wow, this is lovely," Radar noted.

"Yeah, and that's why she loved it here," Sammy murmured.

She hopped out, and he stepped to her door and said, "Hey, hang on a minute. This isn't just a walk in the park right now."

"No, it sure isn't," she confirmed. "Unfortunately my skills are much more of an advantage on a computer, much less on something like this."

"I didn't even know there were any extrasensory skills that you could use on a computer."

She smiled at him. "Think about really gifted musicians, how they can make their instruments sing." He nodded. "Same thing," she muttered. "That's what I do with computers."

"Okay." And he just left it at that.

She pulled his arm gently, then pointed off to the side. "That's the area where she used to spend time."

"And you know that how?"

"Photos. And, no, not photos that most people would access."

"Is that why Johnny asked you to help him?"

"Probably, but, as I mentioned before, we go way back."

"Yet I feel something else is there too. Does he have whatever it is you call woo-woo skills?"

She laughed. "No, and he does find my skills kind of scary."

"As in scary good?"

She shrugged. "I don't really talk to him about it. He's very religious, and this stuff would be considered very uncool."

"Would he stop talking to you if he found out about it?"

"I don't know, and I'm hoping to never put that to the test."

"Right. Let's hope we don't have to. In the meantime, I want to go take a walk around this area."

"What will this area show you?" she asked curiously, as she fell into step beside him.

"I'm not sure, but what I can tell you is that, sitting in that vehicle and listening to you, it was getting to me. So this is a far better option. Besides, I do a lot of things by feel."

"Exactly, just like Gage. Did you know he's got these *probe thingys?*"

At that he stopped and frowned at her. "*Probe thingys?*"

"Yeah, probes. He mentally, psychically, however, feels the area around him. I've seen them, but I basically batted them away from me."

"Okay, do you want to tell me why?"

"Because I wasn't sure what Gage sent his probe looking for. I figured they were to check me out to make sure I was safe to do whatever I needed to do with you guys—because he appears to be all about ..." She stopped, thought about it, and smiled. "Being a guardian."

"It's a really good name for them."

"I think he was just checking to confirm I was safe."

"So why didn't you just let him do whatever he wanted to do with the probe?"

She smiled. "I basically told the probe it was all good."

"And he accepted that?"

"Gage didn't come back to me with another one, so I presume so."

"Man, I have *so* got to have a talk with that guy," Radar stated indignantly.

"Yeah, you do that," she agreed, chuckling. "Let me know how it turns out."

AS RADAR AND Sammy walked, Radar's mind churned, both with the job at hand and with her words. She had heard something about Terk, and so much that he was largely unaware of. Levi hadn't shared much, just that, if Radar decided to stay and work for Terk on a regular basis, Radar could learn a lot. That just made him wonder if Levi had some idea about Radar's internal radar or his instincts.

He'd often wondered why his parents had given him such a nickname. It had been fun and unique growing up, but, at the same time, he'd wondered. His mom had been incredibly intuitive, and she used to smile at him and say that he'd inherited her gift, which is why intuition was okay. She had passed away when Radar was only eight, and his father had remarried. All mention of his mother had ceased at that point.

His new stepmom had been incredibly insecure and couldn't tolerate having Radar's mother's name brought up all the time. That had been hard for him and with it died any and all mention of intuition or of being like her. His father had never brought it up either.

Radar shook his head, coming back to the present, as he studied the area. They walked over to the spot Sammy had pointed out, wondering whether a man would choose to blow up a place that his daughter had loved or blow up the place where his daughter had died.

As somebody who had lost a mother, Radar could see both, depending on how he was doing in his own mental space at the moment. In Radar's case, he would want to memorialize where his mother had passed on, but that was a hospital and made no sense to him. So instead he'd spent a lot of time at her favorite haunts. Now that was something that he could get behind.

As they walked at a pace designed to look like a stroll, he knew that his so-called stroll was a bit on the fast side. He pulled her back slightly and whispered, "We need to slow it down a bit."

She did, and he grabbed her hand. When she frowned at him, Radar added, "Just trying to look like a couple on a stroll."

She nodded and settled back even slower. "In that case, we really should take our time."

"Why? Do you like going out on walks?" he asked in a teasing tone of voice, even as his gaze continued to search the area.

"Always," she replied. "It was one of my favorite pastimes. Hence why Johnny and I are so close. He accepts me. He feels like family."

"*Was?*"

She shrugged. "Remember that part about I don't have a partner?"

"Right, and was there a reason behind that?" he asked curiously.

"There's always a reason," she declared, with a smile. "Doesn't mean that anybody understands it though."

"Try me."

She studied him, then shrugged. "I'm not sure there's anything to explain really. When you don't fit the norm, you don't fit. It's hard to fit into something that's not you."

"Have you always felt you were an outsider?"

"Always," she confirmed. "Just never seems to be another group of people like me."

"Maybe not. It's not necessarily wrong or bad though, is it?"

"No, just a very strange way to grow up," she shared.

"My mother passed away when I was eight," he said abruptly. "She was very intuitive."

"Ah, so *intuition* is a word you're okay with. It's probably something that she used."

He nodded. "Yep, that's true. However, after her death, it's not a word I was ever allowed to use because my stepmom was a fairly insecure person. My mom's name wasn't even allowed to be spoken. It's as if she ceased to exist. And so did intuition."

"Did you get along with your stepmom?"

"I got along with her as well as anybody, considering the situation," he noted. "I would have preferred my own mother, but it wasn't to be. So it was nice to not necessarily be alone at least, and she made my dad happy. It was weird not to talk about my mom or anything."

"Of course," Sammy agreed. "Deaths are hard on everybody, but I think, for the children, it's way worse."

"I would agree, but my father suffered terribly as well.

They were definitely lovebirds."

"Did your stepmom know your mother?"

"Yes, they'd been friends."

"Right. So, if the stepmom knew about that deeply intuitive side of your mother, the second wife may not have been able to handle that, seeing it as just more competition, more comparison, less acceptance of her. It would be easier on her if none of that was ever brought up."

"My dad mentioned something about it at the time, and believe me, I haven't mentioned it. I wasn't a big fan of his second marriage, but, at that point, I was already eleven or twelve, I guess. Yeah, so it was a tough couple years for me. They had more family eventually, more kids, so I have two half-siblings, brothers," he said, with a smile. "But I don't really have much of anything to do with the family."

"I think that's another common factor, when there is a death in the family," she noted, with empathy. "Once you leave, it's as if they have a whole world unto themselves that you don't belong in."

"I belonged at one time," he stated. "I belonged while it was my mother's world, but, once it became my stepmother's world, not so much."

She nodded and pointed to a bench. "The pictures I've seen appear to come from that area, like that bench, as if Frenchie sat there and watched his daughter."

They walked over to the bench and then passed it by because an older man sat there on his phone. They stopped not far away, and Radar assessed the area and nodded. "That would make sense. If it's a family spot, and he loved it here, this is where you would sit, if something was going on." Radar could see it in his mind and could understand how someone sitting here could see teams or individuals, coaches and trainers, all the activity. The park was vast, but this area in particular looked to have a very concentrated area of activity.

Just then she nudged him to move forward. As they walked on, she whispered, "I think that's him."

He turned and stared at her. "What?"

"I think that's Frenchie, the old man sitting there," she repeated in a low tone.

Casually Radar turned to look behind them and saw the old man sitting there, still on the phone. "Seriously?"

There was absolutely nothing dangerous looking about him, but, as Radar well knew, particularly when it came to bomb makers, they could be very hands off, dangerous as hell, yet look like your neighborhood milkman. In this particular case, the old man looked sick and tired. "It could be."

"What do we do then?" she asked, worried.

"That's a good question because how do we find out? We can wait and see where he goes and what he does, but ..." It was a shitty option. Radar's mind raced, trying to figure out what their choices were. He could sit down beside Frenchie, but, if he already had any bombs set up, Frenchie could just walk away, not leading them anywhere important or relevant. Or Frenchie could just take himself out, leaving them with nothing but questions. Radar looked over at her. "How can you be sure?"

"I can't," she claimed, "not here. Not now." She faced Radar and suggested, "You really need to expand those *instincts* of yours. I bet you can pick up on him." Radar frowned at her, and she stated firmly, "Just send out a probe, the way Gage does."

"Yeah, if I even knew what that meant, I could try it,"

Radar replied in disgust. He pulled out his phone and quickly texted Gage. When there was no immediate response, he phoned. Finally Gage answered.

"Hey."

"Where are you?" Radar asked.

"We're heading to another safe house, and you were right. Just as we left, another vehicle drove up and started firing into the house."

"Great. Glad that my instincts in that moment were correct."

"Yeah," Gage replied in a wry tone. "Me too. Now where are you, and what are you guys up to?"

Radar quickly explained, where they were and why, then added, "Sammy seems to think it might be him."

"Right there, sitting beside you?"

"Yeah. We're a good one hundred yards behind and tucked up out of sight, as we try and figure out what our options are." He hesitated, then said, "This guy does look pretty sick, like he's about done."

"The problem is, if you take him down, and he doesn't cooperate, any and all information he has with him would go with him too."

"Exactly, but, at the same time, it's almost as if he's here, saying goodbye or something."

"Which then would mean that the plaza *was* potentially the target?"

"That's what I don't know."

At that, Sammy pulled her arm free and whispered, "I'll be right back." She raced off, and, even as Radar watched in shock, she walked up calmly as you please and sat down on the same bench with the old man.

When Frenchie turned and looked at her, she just smiled

and turned to look at the scenes all around her.

"Jesus," Radar grumbled, "she just walked over and sat down beside him."

"Who did?" Gage asked.

"Sammy," he said in frustration. "We couldn't figure out any way to confirm whether it was him or not."

"So, what will this move of hers do?"

"I have no idea, except maybe blow our cover."

"What cover?" Gage asked, with a snort. "We're all rather desperate to get a hold of this man and to figure out what the hell he's got planned."

"I still don't know that this is the best way to go about it," Radar grumbled.

"I don't think it matters anymore," Gage noted. "It's the hand you've been dealt."

CHAPTER 10

SAMMY SAT IN the lovely afternoon sun, tilted her head up to the sky, and just let the heat hit her face.

"My daughter used to do that," the man beside her said gruffly.

She looked over at him and smiled. "It's lovely to enjoy temperatures like this. The feel of the sun is special."

"She's dead," he snapped, his mood going from one to the other almost instantly.

"I'm sorry," Sammy replied. "Sometimes what we want for our children isn't how it ends up." He didn't say anything to that. She looked over at him and realized that he really did look very sick. His skin was sallow, patchy, and he looked exhausted. She murmured, "Are you okay?" When he just stared at her, she shrugged. "You seem to not be in very good health yourself."

"I'm not. … Not getting any better either."

She hesitated before speaking. "I don't know if this is a good thing to say or not," she began carefully, "but at least then you will see your daughter soon."

He stared at her; then he slowly smiled. "Yes. Yes, I will. It's what keeps me going."

"Good," she whispered. "And that's the thing, isn't it? To do what you need to do, so you can go see her, knowing she's been watching over you all this time." He stared at her, his gaze narrowing. She shrugged. "At least that's what I like to think, that all our family members and friends are there just waiting for us, watching over us. Maybe it's fanciful, but it makes me feel better," she admitted.

His shoulders sagged ever-so-slightly.

"You don't think so?" she asked, keeping to a casual curious tone.

He shook his head. "I want to think that she's been looking over my shoulder all this time," he replied, "but maybe it's better if she wasn't."

"Ah. Regrets can be a tough thing to live with too," she murmured.

He stared at her, once again with that lightning-fast change of expression.

She smiled at him. "When we do things that we think they wouldn't like, the thought of them watching us can be disconcerting. It used to bother me thinking that my brother was potentially seeing me when I was having a bath or when I was out with boyfriends and doing things I shouldn't be, … like drinking," she explained, with a laugh.

He shook his head. "To have regrets is to have done wrong in the first place. I did nothing wrong."

"Good for you," she stated, unperturbed. "I am not so blameless." But that gaze of his wouldn't let up. She turned to face him. "At least I don't think I am," she murmured, with a shrug. "I have lived a normal life and have not always been the best that I could be, but my intent was always good."

"Intentions are everything," he claimed, as he stared at the park. "My daughter? … She loved it here."

"It's a beautiful spot. A place of laughter, a place of joy. I'm so glad that it's here for everybody. Of course I also really like the big city square. That's another place of great joy." She knew she was taking a chance, bringing up the area where they thought the bombing was being planned.

"Great joy? Why do you think that?" he asked, staring at her with that odd flat look again.

"Because it's a place of a meeting of the minds. It's a place of questions and answers, a place of communication," she explained calmly. "It's a place where people can join in and can know that they are free to be themselves. If your daughter loved it here, I'm sure she would have loved it there as well."

He stiffened at that. "She did love it, but it doesn't matter. It works."

"It works, yes. It's functional," she agreed, "but it's more than that because a lot of people really love it and enjoy being there." When he didn't say anything, she smiled and looked at him hesitantly. "Have you spent much time there?"

"No," he replied, his tone flat. "It's not my place."

She looked confused at that comment. "If your daughter enjoyed it, why don't you spend time there as well?"

"It serves its purpose," he stated. Then he stiffened, as pain crossed his features.

She leaned forward and then settled back at the look on his face. "Can I get someone to help you?"

He shook his head. "There is no one. They have all gone before me."

"Then your time coming up should be one of joy."

"It will be," he declared, "and vengeance is mine." And, with that, he straightened up taller in his seat.

"Is vengeance really how you want to go out of life?" she asked him. "There are so many other options."

"No, there are no other options. Everything, ... everything I loved was taken from me."

She nodded. "I'm so sorry for that because so much more exists in life than focusing on all the bad."

"Really?" he asked, with a laugh. "You are such a child."

"And with a child comes a childlike sense of questioning and innocence," she responded. "The world is an ugly place, but, if you only focus on all the dark things, you only know darkness."

"When the darkness hits you, and you have no choice but to focus on it, you then realize that you've been looking for unicorns the whole time, in a place where none exist."

She winced at that. "I always thought unicorns were a good thing."

He just glared at her.

"I get it. It's not a good thing, and it's not what you would want for yourself. Wishes that don't come true. Dreams that never materialized. Hopes that stayed at a fantasy level and never became goals"—she stared straight ahead—"but life doesn't always have to be that way."

"Who are you?" he demanded, his tone rough. "Why are you here?"

She motioned at the park around her. "I'm here with my boyfriend, enjoying this wonderful place."

"And the boyfriend? Where is he?" Frenchie asked, looking around.

"He got caught up on the phone," she shared, with a laugh. "Business, it's always business."

"It's required," he said. "Sometimes business is necessary."

"Business is almost always necessary, but taking a break, relishing the time that we have, taking time to enjoy life, and, yes, honoring those who have gone before us, those things are also important."

He shook his head. "You and I don't think the same way when it comes to honor."

"Maybe not because, to me, honor means not hurting somebody else. Honor means living my life to the fullest, with accountability for my actions."

"What about other people's actions?" he snapped, his voice hard, flat. "What about their actions when they don't do so well?"

"That is just the way of the world, isn't it?" she noted, knowing that it would be almost impossible to get through to him, but Sammy was incapable of not trying. She could only hope that everybody else was doing what they needed to do, but she was here with Frenchie, talking to him and thinking there might be a chance of changing his mind and turning him from this final act of destruction. It was something she didn't dare *not* attempt.

"There are so many good things in life, and, even though you're hurting, do you really think that this is how your daughter would want you to meet her? Is this how she would want to see you spend your last few days?"

"You know nothing about it."

"No, of course I don't," she admitted, looking at him. "And I can't know anything of it if you don't tell me. So, why not tell me?"

"I'm not telling you anything," he snapped.

She nodded. "Understood. I'm sorry for your loss. If I could help in some way, I would."

He stared at her. "It makes no sense that you would help."

"I don't think so," she murmured. "It's hard to watch other people hurt."

"It's not hard. It's mandatory. An eye for an eye."

She winced at that. "Yet, it's really not the same people who are ever affected, is it?"

"This time it will be," he snapped. "This time it will. Then I go to my maker. I go see my family, and all will be well." Then he got up and started to walk back over to his truck.

She called out, "But will it? Will your daughter be happy to see you? With what you're doing, will your daughter be happy? Will she understand why are you so focused on vengeance? Or would she prefer that you walk in silence in the world, finding joy in the happy moments and remembering the good things about life?"

He stopped, then stared at her with such an ugly look on his face that it made her stop in her tracks. "You know nothing. I will have my answers."

"Answers or results?" she questioned.

He glared at her. "Results … and that works for me just fine. There is nothing more to be asked of this world. There was only hardship and pain and nobody who answered for it. There is no justice, so I am making my own. My daughter's death was wholly unnecessary, and there was nobody to look after her. There was nobody to help her. There was nobody to make them pay, so now I will do it myself."

She shook her head. "Do you think that is the only answer?"

"I know who you are," he cried out.

"Who am I?" she asked.

He stopped, confused, then shrugged. "You're somebody from the police. I don't know how you found me or what you know, but you can't say anything that will make me change my mind."

"I got that," she said, "and it makes me very sad because your daughter is watching. Your daughter is there, listening."

"Good. Then, if she understands her papa, she'll know perfectly well that I'm doing what I always intended on doing, and, when that is done, I'm coming to her. All of this is for her."

"Only she won't necessarily be there," Sammy noted. "Your daughter is purity and light and innocence. She is all the good things in our world, so what makes you think you will go where she is?"

He stared at her, his face working. "Because my God is not so angry," he declared. "My God understands. Your God does not."

"Maybe not," she admitted.

"They can do what they will with my body when I am gone," he said. "I care not. I only care about making sure they pay."

"Who is *they*?" she asked, not moving from her spot. When he looked at her, she asked, "Whoever killed your daughter, did they not pay?"

"No, they did not, but he will now."

"What if it was an accident?"

"It was no accident. It was incompetence."

She replied, "Ah, and you believe that incompetence deserves a fatal punishment."

"Of course. When you make mistakes with the lives of people, the consequences should be severe." He looked at her. "I'm too old to care, and my mind is set. If you were trying to stop me, it's already too late."

She nodded. "I was just trying to understand the man behind it all."

"Why do you care?"

"Because you'll go down in history as a monster. It would be much nicer to understand how such a monster came about."

"A monster? Am I?" Then he laughed. "I can live with that. At least on my side of life, this monster has done right by his family." And, with that, he stumbled forward to his vehicle.

She knew he wouldn't get very far because, for one thing, Radar was somewhere around. She followed at a calm pace behind him. When he got to his vehicle, he pulled out a gun from inside the car and turned it her way.

She stopped, looked at it, and nodded. "Didn't like the questions, *huh*?"

"It's not the questions," he clarified. "I just don't want anybody to stop my last plans."

"You mean, killing the poor officer who hasn't been able to stand his own life all this time because of the guilt he feels for accidentally killing a child? Would it not be much more painful for him to be left alive to continue to suffer each day, like he has?"

He stared at her. "He doesn't suffer enough."

"Oh, I think he does," she argued. "He suffers terribly for what he did. It was his bullet, and it was his job to keep everyone safe. Back then, not knowing what would happen, he chose to shoot, trying to stop the shooter from hurting someone. Instead his own bullet hurt someone, not just someone but an innocent child. It was an accident, a terrible accident, but he has been riddled with guilt, taking responsibility for his actions. However, I guess for you, it doesn't matter. In your mind, he still deserves to die."

"He does deserve to die," he cried out. "Just like my little girl."

"She deserved to die?" she questioned.

He frowned at her. "No, of course not."

"Right, it was an accident."

"Yes, no, it wasn't …" He frowned. "Stop it now. You're making me confused. Just stop. … Stop it."

"I'm not trying to make you confused. I'm questioning whether this is you really doing this because of your daughter or just you choosing to avoid death by cancer with a faster send-off," she explained. "It will make a difference in the way history views you."

"Revenge is important to me," he stated.

"Nobody could help her," Sammy reminded him.

"Nobody even tried to help her, and she was left on the street."

"She was already dead," Sammy told him. "You know that."

He shook his head. "No, I don't know that. Nobody stopped to help her."

Sammy already knew that to be incorrect. "That is also a lie. People went to help her, but there was nothing that anybody could do."

"Go away," he said. "I'm tired, and I don't want you here."

"That's nice," she noted, "but you've set bombs in the plaza just around the corner from here, and, for all I know, you're planning on blowing up this place too."

He looked at her, then smiled. "You'll never know," he remarked easily. "You talk to me like you know something, but you don't know anything. You know nothing, and that's because I don't share. I don't wish to share it. This is my life, not yours."

"It is, indeed," she agreed sadly. "So you will go down in

history as one of those monsters, one of those religiously misguided souls."

He stared at her, his jaw working, and then he shook his head. "It doesn't matter. My life is already over. I'm riddled with cancer, and there's nothing they can do about it. Maybe it was the rotting of my soul that brought me to this. I don't know, but it matters not. I'll go to God with a clean soul after this."

"You think so?" she asked, with a sad smile. "Do you not realize that, if I'm here, they're working hard to clear the plaza right now?"

He stared at her and nodded. "I'm sure they are, but they won't find it."

"Why is that?"

Just then, he grabbed at his chest, his heart cramping, as he cried out in pain, dropping to his knees.

She raced to his side and kicked away the gun. "Help us," she pleaded. "Don't do this. You don't need to take all those people to their deaths too."

"I have to," he stated. "Justice is mine."

"No," she disagreed, as she checked his pulse. "That's not justice at all. That's just hate."

"It matters not." Then he cried out once again and slowly dropped, his face turning bloodred.

She pulled apart his shirt, only to realize Radar was here, checking Frenchie over. "I think it's already too late," she whispered.

Radar had already phoned for ambulance. "I think you're right," he agreed. "I'll get started with CPR, but it seems to be a full-on heart attack."

"There's no pulse, at least not one strong enough for me to feel." She sat back on her heels and stared at Frenchie.

"He was so angry, so hurt."

"Yet he was there at the same time of his daughter's death, so what you want to bet it was the guilt? This was all because of the guilt he felt because he couldn't stop it. Much like Johnny with his uncle's death."

"I wouldn't be at all surprised," Sammy acknowledged. "It's usually something very simple."

"Yet the death of a loved one is anything but." Radar lifted his face to her. "It's one of the hardest, most complicated emotions for people to deal with."

"Of course it is, and I don't mean to nullify or to degrade that in any way, but I don't think his heart was necessarily set on this. I think it was a pathway he felt he had to follow, and, in his mind, there was really no other choice."

Just then Radar's phone rang. He tossed it to her, and she answered and put it on Speaker. "Yeah, Gage. Frenchie's gone down, probably with a heart attack. CPR in progress."

Radar quickly explained what had happened before that. "She tried to talk him out of it, tried to get him to explain why and what and where, but he wasn't having any of it. Still, I think she touched him in some way. It just wasn't enough." He turned and looked at her, while speaking mostly to Gage. "We'll check Frenchie's truck and check him for anything, any clue. I'm worried about the cop. We haven't been to his place yet. Once the ambulance gets here, we'll go over there next."

"I can send somebody else if you want," Gage offered.

"No, once the ambulance is here, we'll talk to them for a minute. Then we'll race over there ourselves." Once the paramedics arrived, he quickly transitioned the CPR to them and told the EMT to phone Gage for more details.

"Our patient is MI6's bomb maker? The bomb maker

they're clearing the plaza for?"

The explanation wasn't an easy one, and Radar had a hard time getting free, reminding them again to call Gage for details. With that out of his hair, Radar dragged Sammy by the arm. "Let's go." Then they raced to the rental vehicle.

As they hopped in, she was unusually quiet.

"Did he get to you?" Radar asked her.

"He was just a broken, sick old man. He was grieving, and, by the end, he was doing what he thought he could do. All he could think about was pushing that pain and hurt onto other people."

"Yeah," Radar noted, "that's not exactly unusual."

"No, but it's so unnecessary," she said, looking at him sadly. "There are so many other things in life that people could do, so many other things they could be, and yet Frenchie chose to take out as many people as he could. That doesn't sound like a good deal for any of us."

Radar punched the address of the cop's home into the GPS and quickly followed the directions. "We're just looking to make sure that he's here and that he's safe."

"I'm also not sure that Frenchie was alone."

"Not exactly what we want to hear, but let's deal with this first. I haven't had an update on the plaza either."

"Seems everything is so up in the air at the moment." At that, her phone rang. "Johnny, what's happening?"

RADAR LISTENED WITH half an ear to her conversation, as he pulled into the driveway in front of the cop's house. He had the cop's phone number, and Radar called it again, but, so far, every time he called, he got no answer, and that was not a good sign. He looked over at her, still on the phone with Johnny.

"I'm coming. I'm coming." She quickly hung up the phone, hopped out of the vehicle. and raced with Radar inside the building, now climbing the stairs. She asked, "Why not the elevator?"

He shrugged. "Instincts."

"Good enough," she said, even with an eyeroll.

"Did Johnny have any news?"

"The bomb squad is there, looking. Plus Jonas sidelined Andy. He's now under investigation as yet another mole."

Radar nodded as he raced down the hallway, until he found the apartment. He quickly knocked on the door, and, when there was no answer, he looked at her. "You're not seeing this." Then he pulled out his tools and quickly unlocked the door. He raced inside and stopped.

He turned, motioned her out, and stepped back out again. He pulled out his phone and called Gage. "The cop is dead. I'll leave Sammy in the hallway, then go in and take a quick look. You need to call the police." And, with that, he stepped into the apartment. When he turned, she was there with him, a determined look on her face.

"If he's dead, nothing I can do to help him," she stated, "but maybe, maybe … there's something from the bomb maker here."

At that, Radar's phone rang again, and this time it was Jonas. "No bomb is here," he spat in frustration. "What's this about the bomb maker going to the hospital?"

"I don't have time to explain, but we met him at the park, and he had a heart attack. They took him off in an ambulance, but I would be stunned if they brought him around. Now we're at the home of the cop who shot

Frenchie's daughter accidentally, and we've got a dead body here."

Jonas started to swear fluently on the other end of the call.

"I get it," Radar said. "I'll call you back in a few minutes, after we have a chance to search and to see if there are any clues, but I suspect not." Radar hit Speaker.

"Maybe, but where the hell is the bomb? Are you sure that he was looking to take out this location?"

"Yes," Sammy answered. "I'm pretty sure. I spoke with him for a good ten or fifteen minutes, and he's all about misplaced justice. He's all about revenge."

"Fine, but if you don't have a way for us to find it, and it goes off—"

"Yeah, I know, and it'll go off today."

"Are you sure?"

"Yes, I'm sure. There was just something about the way he spoke. Frenchie knew he was done. He knew this was all over, and it was his last shot," she murmured. "Are you sure no bomb is there?"

"No bomb is here," Jonas repeated.

"Okay, then go to the park and check. I was there, but it's a vast place."

"But why there? Not that many people will be there."

"Is there any game slated, any practices, anything?" she asked.

"I'll find out." And he hung up.

She quickly followed Radar into the bedroom, and there was the cop. He was lying on his back, fully dressed in his uniform, with a bullet hole right in the forehead, between his eyes. Handwritten on the wall above his head were the words *You're too late.*

That made his heart slam in fury. "Godammit," Radar growled.

"The trouble is, it's not just that we're too late for this guy," she pointed out. "Frenchie's trying to say we're too late for all of it."

"This man has been dead for hours, if not days," Radar stated in a fury. "So how long has this final big event for Frenchie been going on?"

"He's been building up to this, and that's the problem. Now we have to figure out exactly where his revenge bomb is."

"If they're looking at the park, that's a good thing."

"Only if they can keep the park shut down."

As they headed back outside, Jonas called back. "There's a huge celebrity ball game going on," he shared, "so the park will be full. We're talking thousands of people there."

"Guess what? You need to cancel it, and you need to cancel it now," she barked into the phone. "And get the bomb squad over there and make sure nothing's going on."

"Yeah, wouldn't that be nice, but I have to regroup and get them moved from here first."

"But you don't have time," she said. "Even while we were there at that park, a crowd was starting to gather. That's why Frenchie got up to leave. I'm sure of it."

"Dammit," Jonas swore. Once again, Jonas hung up.

She looked at the phone, then at Radar. "I guess we better go back and help."

"What help are you planning to give him? The place is crawling with people, not to mention the danger of bombs going off, and it's a huge park to search so late into this event."

"I know, and that's why we have to help. Let's go." And,

with that, she led the way, racing down the stairs.

Radar wanted to stay until the cops arrived at least, but there was nothing they could do for the dead cop. He was already long gone, and the best thing Radar could do was to try and find a way to snag that bomb before anybody stumbled over it.

The trouble was, he had no idea where it was.

As he drove them back to the park, she asked, "Do you have any idea where he'd hide the bomb?"

"Why would I have that?" When she looked at him with a flat expression, he groaned. "Ah, you're back to that internal radar stuff, aren't you?"

"Yep, I sure am," she stated, "and honestly I think you are our best bet."

"In that case we've lost already," he replied, his tone harsh. "It's one thing to do the work I do and to have the instincts I do, but it's another thing entirely to have somebody depending on me to pull the location of a fucking bomb out of thin air," he snapped.

"Look. I get it. This is frustrating and making you angry because you don't really understand what I'm asking of you, but I think, if you open your eyes and open your heart, … you'll understand."

"Maybe," he grumbled, "but I'm sure as hell not there right now."

She smiled. "You've got at least five minutes to get yourself ready." He looked at her, startled, and she shrugged. "The park is coming up. It'll be at the next set of turns, and then it's no longer practice time. Radar, … this is D day," she declared. "It's now or never because we'll be at the park ourselves, and, depending on where Frenchie's got this bomb placed—and only one bomb, we hope—it'll be bad news for everybody, including us."

He parked off to the side and turned off the engine. Sammy raced out of the truck and ran over to where the bomb maker had been sitting earlier. She sat down on the bench. "What are you doing?" Radar asked, coming up behind her.

"He was sitting here, staring over that way. So, why is that?"

"Let's go find out," he said. With that, he picked up the pace and started to run in that direction. Huge bleachers were set up, and even more were being pulled out for tonight's event. "We don't know about thousands of people, like Jonas had suggested, but there will definitely be many hundreds of people affected, if a bomb went off here. Depending on the size of the bomb, the casualties would be way more." As he raced toward the setup, he saw the bomb squad and police coming toward him, telling him to get the hell out of the park.

He shook his head. "We're here at Jonas's request." They looked at him with a blank expression, and Radar added, "MI6." With that, they just stepped aside, and he kept on going. He looked to see where Sammy was, but she'd been stopped behind him and was even now being escorted to the far side of the park.

"Good enough," he muttered under his breath because that was at least one less person for Radar to worry about. One less person for him to try to keep safe. He headed over to the side, then he stopped and looked around.

A member of the bomb squad searched the area.

Radar pointed in a particular direction and asked, "Have you checked up there?"

"Yeah, we sure have."

"What's the maximum amount of destruction he could do with a bomb here?"

The guy looked at him and replied, "Honestly it's hard to say. If it's chemical, it could be anywhere—in the irrigation system even," he noted, as he turned to look around. "Think maximum destruction." The bomb expert looked at him. "If it's chemical, then we're really in trouble because it could possibly go anywhere, even into the sprinkler system." He pointed to the maintenance shed nearby.

Radar nodded. "Let's check the timer, and see when it's set to come on." With that, the guy hesitated, so Radar asked, "Have you got another idea?"

"No, I don't. We've been searching this place for the last forty minutes, and nobody has turned up anything."

"And that's why we're here right now," Radar stated. "The park is about to get very busy."

"I hope not. They're supposed to be stopping the crowds."

"You'll only stop them for so long, and then it'll be an absolute shit show out there, as the crowd decides to push back. You know how it goes."

The bomb squad guy nodded. "I do." As they headed toward the maintenance shed, he said, "This is too far out to really be anything, but …" Then he stopped.

"What about under all these bleachers?" Radar asked.

"I've checked them all," he replied.

"Do they all come out automatically?"

He nodded. "They come out and fold up on their own."

"Okay, so what about the actual control center for the bleachers."

"Let's go take a look at that too," he agreed. "They're pretty close together. I wish we hadn't mentioned chemicals though."

"It's not his usual MO, so I don't know. All I can tell you is that Frenchie is one hell of a danger to all of us." Radar led the way through the maintenance area and then headed over to the mechanical side. He pointed to a small flashing light.

The bomb expert swore. "I didn't see that before, and I don't think it was flashing. I was just looking in this direction, but now I see it clearly, so it seems to have just started."

"Shit." They raced over, took a quick look, found one wire. They tracked the wire, and it went halfway across the room to another small brace. "This is all part of the mechanics that control the bleachers, right?"

"Yes."

"So, if this goes off while the bleachers are full?"

"Yeah, well, you'll not only have people affected by the blast but the bleachers themselves are super high and metal. So, if they shatter, people will fall. Plus, with metal shards all over the place, we're talking hundreds if not thousands of injuries."

"Which is what he's after," Radar shared. "Can you stop it?"

"I have to figure it out first," he mumbled, and, with that, he sent out an alert to the rest of his team. The bomb tech looked over at him. "You need to leave."

"Yeah, I'm not good at leaving a deal like this, not if there's anything I can do to help."

"We're out of time right now."

Then Radar saw another wire. "Is this one connected?" It took the two of them a good twenty minutes just to figure out that not only were the mechanics in here set to blow but it also would trigger blasts set up inside the buried irrigation system that would directly impact teams on the fields. Radar swore as he looked at that. "This place will get demolished, both players and onlookers alike."

At that, the rest of the bomb disposal team raced up, when they saw what was going on, Radar was quickly ushered out to the front. But there was no front anymore, and the place was deserted, except for a few cops who were directing people. He warned them, "The whole place is set to blow, and I have no idea whether the bomb techs will stop it or not."

At that, one of the cops nodded. "Let's go. Everybody out of here," he called out. "Be sensible and safe. Get back and let them do their job."

Radar thought about it, then nodded.

The same cop said, "That's all fine, but I'm wondering if the guy who set this up is still around here somewhere."

"No, he's in hospital." Then Radar swore. "I shouldn't be telling you that."

"That's okay. I was there when he had the heart attack," he stated. "Still I wonder if anybody else is here who could be recording this."

"Recording this?" Radar repeated.

"Yeah, you know how these guys like to take claim. Even if the bomb maker's dead, I'm sure he would want somebody to make sure this went off as planned."

At that, one of the cops turned, looked around, and mentioned, "I caught a guy on the other side with a video camera. He was pretty insistent about staying, and I thought he was with the news media or something."

"Not likely," Radar stated. "Let's go see if we can find him."

At that, the cop looked around, picked up the pace, and

ran toward where he'd last seen him. "His vehicle is still there, but I see no sign of him."

"Which means he's here somewhere, looking for the best spot, and wherever he is, that will be the safest place here because he's in cahoots with the bomb maker." Which meant it was likely one of the two men who had kidnapped Sammy and Johnny, and Radar would love to find that asshole. "So, in that case, we need to catch him and catch him fast." Then he heard somebody shouting his name. He turned, and there was Sammy, calling out for him.

She raced up to him and the cop and said, "We've got to get out of here."

"But I think somebody here is part of it all. Somebody set to take pictures of it, so he can post it and maybe make a video out of it. Likely one of your kidnappers."

"God, that's just sick."

"In a worst-case scenario, he's got a fail-safe," Radar murmured.

She stared at him in shock and then nodded, along with the cop. "That makes more sense. As long as he's here, he can see whether it happens or not."

"Exactly," Radar agreed. "So we need to find him. This cop saw somebody with a camera not very long ago."

She nodded. "Yeah, he headed over on that side." She pointed to the fields on the far side, where there was a bunch of trees. "What do you want to bet he's trying to find himself a spot high up in the trees, where he'll be safe."

"I don't think anybody will be safe. Wait right here."

"Like hell," she snapped, as he turned to her. "I don't need you to tell me that. I'm in for the long haul—in case you hadn't figured that out."

"Yeah, well, I'm not sure what the long haul is in this

case," he growled, pissed that she wouldn't listen.

"Yeah? You'll figure it out eventually."

He frowned at her, shrugging at the cop.

"Don't worry about it right now. If you haven't figured out your internal radar shit, you sure as hell haven't figured this out."

He groaned, as the three of them ran. "Why is everything so complicated with you?"

"Because you keep ignoring what's right in front of you."

"What? My radar?"

"Yeah, your radar," she snapped, "and something else."

"Yeah? You want to tell me what that something else is?"

"Nope. You'll have to figure that out for yourself."

"Doesn't seem that'll happen." The three of them reached the tree line, barely catching their breath. Radar reached out and grabbed the cop's arm. "We have to be careful, since odds are that he's armed."

At that, the cop pulled his own weapon. "Yeah, I hear you there, but if he's got a fail-safe or a backup plan, we need to put a stop to it."

Just as they went to take a step forward, a shot rang out and hit a tree right beside them.

"Bingo."

His face grim, the cop nodded and pulled out his phone, quickly speaking to somebody on the other end. He looked over at Radar. "We've been told to pull back."

At that, Radar shook his head. "No, I'm pretty sure our gunman's got a second trigger up there, for sure. I don't know for what, but I'm pretty certain, if this doesn't blow the way it's been set up, he's got a secondary option." The cop looked at him. Radar nodded. "Take her, and both of you head on out of here. I'll be out in a minute, but I need to check."

"That won't work," she stated. "The shooter's just looking for you so he can pop you one."

"He'll have to find me first and don't think he won't take you out too," he added, giving her a firm look. "Now, either stay here and stay very well hidden or go back with this guy, but I'm doing this alone."

With that, he slipped into the trees, closing his eyes and using the one thing he had always been able to count on all these years. He used his senses to sort out where this guy was. Almost instantly he sensed him up ahead. Slipping through the trees, Radar kept his own energy low and close to his body, as he moved swiftly in the deep brush.

He heard a voice up ahead. "Yeah, I don't know if I can pull this off. Would you answer your damn phone? I offered to help you, but I didn't expect this. You're supposed to be here. You're supposed to be answering your phone and helping me."

At that, Radar stopped under the tree and looked up. He saw the person in question, trying to make another call. Radar assessed the height of the tree, looking to see if he could possibly climb it quietly. Then he reached for the lowest of the branches and hoisted himself up.

He heard something akin to chanting on the other side, some kind of prayer. When Radar came around the tree trunk and popped right down in front of the shooter, the guy just stared, dropping his phone in shock. "If you're trying to call Frenchie, it's too late," Radar told him.

"What?"

"He's dead."

"No, that's not possible. He can't be."

"He is. He had a heart attack in the parking lot about an hour and a half ago, so if that's who you're trying to call, it won't work."

The young guy stared at him in shock. "It's not possible. It's not possible."

"It's past possible," Radar muttered. "Now you need to talk with the police."

"I'm not going anywhere," he replied. "This has to happen tonight. I have all the sites waiting for the video."

Radar stared at him. "That's what it is to you, just a video?"

"Yeah, we made a deal. He would give me some video that would send my ratings soaring," he murmured. "I need it."

"What about what's in your hand?"

"He told me that, if everything went past a certain time, and it didn't go as planned, to punch this," he explained, then smiled. "So I'll still get the video."

"Is that all you care about?" Radar asked, as he assessed how dangerous this other guy was. But he seemed to be just some kid, some punk looking for cheap thrills to make money and to gain kudos on the internet. "Get down," Radar ordered.

The kid shook his head. "No, I won't."

"You need to. Staying up here is really not an option."

"That's too damn bad. You don't understand. I've already got everybody waiting for the shot and, if I don't do this, I'll be ruined."

Radar stared at him. "And you realize, if one person, even one person dies today, you'll be up for murder, right?"

He shook his head. "He told me that I would be free and clear."

"Sure, I'll bet Frenchie said a lot of things, but he didn't tell you that he was really sick, did he?"

"Sure he did," he scoffed. "I didn't need to be told anyway. It was obvious he was dying."

"Yeah, and that's what's happened, and now he's not even here to see it."

"It doesn't matter now. It's his legacy, and that was the deal. I can't go back on my word."

"He really got you brainwashed on that, didn't he?"

At that, the kid glared at him. "Who are you to even speak to me about something like that?" he roared.

"If you don't give me that goddamn trigger," Radar growled, "you can bet we'll have a much bigger problem."

"Yeah, well, what will you do? In case you haven't realized it, we're in a damn tree."

"Yep, and it's a long way down, but not enough to kill you when I throw you off," Radar snapped. "Still enough to break something important."

He glared at him. "You don't know what you're talking about. I can just throw this thing, and it'll make a huge boom anyway. It'll go off all on its own. You drop me, it'll go off. So, no matter what you do, it'll go off," he snapped. "Just think about that before you make any sudden moves."

If this wasn't enough stress, a woman spoke down below. "I'm here, so if you want to throw him out of the tree, just go for it. He's also not one of the kidnappers. Too young. He's not important. Personally I'd toss him."

The kid cried out, "What the hell? I have more value than that."

"Nope, you sure don't," Radar disagreed, hating that she was down there and knowing that she was in as much trouble as anybody else right now. "Come on. Let's get down out of this tree, and, if you pop that thing, the repercussions will be endless. I will personally make sure you get charged with multiple counts of murder. You won't be some internet hero. You'll be an internet villain."

The kid looked at him and laughed. "I don't have a problem with that either," he quipped, holding up the device in his hand.

Radar made a lunge, a calculated move made right when his instincts said *move*. Just like that, the kid started to fall. Radar grabbed him by the arm and snapped the device from his hand, then letting the kid drop. He went down hard, screaming the whole way.

CHAPTER 11

OWN BELOW SAMMY yelled, "I've got him here. Have you got it?"

"I do," he confirmed. "Is the kid hurt?"

"No, he's just screaming a lot," she replied in disgust.

Radar laughed, as he made his way quickly to the ground, holding the device carefully in his hand. "Now, let's go," he ordered, jerking the kid to his feet, dragging him back out into the park, where the others were waiting. "Definitely some people want to talk to you."

"I'm not talking to anybody," he retorted, limping. "You threw me out of a tree."

"Did not. Besides, you were trying to blow up this park and everybody in it."

"Was not," he snapped, down to almost monosyllables. "Besides, it's not my deal. It's the old man's deal."

"As I told you, the old man is dead. So his deal now looks a lot like it's become yours."

"Not unless you found everything he did." The kid laughed. "He was cagey, really cagey. He was worried right up to the end that something would happen and that it wouldn't go off as planned. So I know more contingencies are in place. He really thought this through. His work has always been foolproof."

"In that case we still want to talk to you, don't we?"

The cop raced toward them, the same one who had come to the trees with Radar.

Radar held up the device. "This is something the bomb squad needs to deal with. I have no idea where it goes and what it does, but this kid had it in his hand, and I suspect it's a contingency trigger. Besides, I'm not sure that this is the end of it."

The cop frowned at him.

"The kid was here for the videos," Radar explained, making it clear. "Part of the deal he made with the bomb maker. He's got followers lined up for these incredible videos of the park blowing up," Radar stated in disgust. "Believe me. The cost of the lives doesn't matter to this kid at all. It was all about getting those shots and keeping his followers happy."

The cop turned toward the kid, his face grim as he spoke. "He'll get something to look at from now on, don't worry," he declared. "We've got the bomb squad going crazy in there. They found the bombs," he said.

"There were more?" Sammy asked.

"Yeah, it looks to be over," the cop added.

"I'm not so sure about that," Radar stated. "Still too many uncertainties going on right now."

At that, the cop nodded. "I agree with you there, but, short of having anything else to go on, what else can we do?"

At that, Radar looked over at the kid and saw the smirk on his face. "My instincts say something else is happening." Just as the words came out of his mouth, a drone flew overhead, and then came a spatting sound.

The kid beside him dropped to his knees, a shocked look on his face, then face planted into the grass. Radar didn't waste any time, and, snatching the gun from the kid's pocket, fired at the drone. It took two shots to send it into a spinning glide. The drone crashed onto the grass nearby. He looked over at the cop and nodded. "As I said, I'm not sure this is over."

They raced to the drone, as other cops ran toward them. Two of the bomb squad team members came over at the same time. Radar handed off the remote device, and then they went to assess the drone. He looked over at Sammy, as she smiled.

"See? All found because of that lovely set of instincts of yours."

"Exactly that," he quipped.

She laughed. "Whatever."

"But your version of instincts and mine are two different things."

"You're still a handy guy to have around."

"Why the hell don't you listen when you're told to go stay somewhere safe?"

"Because it wasn't all that hard to track your energy to the tree," she admitted, "and, since it's one thing that I've learned to do cyberwise, it was interesting to try it and to follow it out in the field too."

"Yeah, and what if this idiot kid had shot you?" he asked, his tone rough.

She looked at him, then smiled. "What? You mean you care? That's nice to hear."

"No, it's not nice to hear," he snapped in exasperation. "I don't know what kind of a game this is to you, but to me? Seeing somebody get blown up or hurt isn't something I want to live with."

Her smile fell away, and she nodded. "Exactly. Now you know why I came to the tree." And, with that, she turned and walked away, leaving him staring behind her.

SAMMY AND RADAR were sitting in the rental car several hours later, still waiting for answers, when Jonas finally got hold of them.

"Hey, we've picked up the drone operator."

"Good, was he behind this?" Radar asked, putting his phone on Speaker.

"He was to be some third or fourth fail-safe. He was paid anonymously, and we've tracked that back to the bomb maker. He also gave us his go-between, so we've picked him up too. He wasn't alone, and both are talking. They were the ones who kidnapped Sammy. So, it looks to be over."

Beside him, Sammy sighed with relief. "Thank God for that," she muttered. "I couldn't envision what my life would be like if we had to keep going on like this."

Since the call was on Speakerphone, Jonas heard her. "No, it seems you're good to go."

"So, does that mean I can go home now?"

"Yeah, I would say so. Johnny has gone already. I sent him to join his family, and hopefully soon you can go back to your lives. There is talk of Johnny and his wife and kids heading straight to the Netherlands."

"Yeah, they were making plans for that while we were in the safe house," she noted.

"I need you to come in and do a debriefing."

"I can do that," she agreed, "but not right now, not tonight. Assuming I get a choice in the matter."

With that, she hung up.

RADAR PULLED THE vehicle in front of her apartment building. "So, how does it feel to be back home?"

She looked over at him and smiled, and he noted the fatigue weighing her down, the hair that desperately needed to be tucked away, the body that desperately needed a relaxing hot shower and, most of all, rest.

"When I wake up in a few days, and I realize this really is all over with, I'll be okay. With everything I've worked for all over God-only-knows how many months," she explained, stifling a yawn, "I know it will eventually feel great, but right now it just feels like crap. I have been down to this one outfit. So shopping, insurance, and so much more needs to be dealt with."

She stumbled getting out of the vehicle, and he quickly hopped over to her side to help. "Easy now."

"I'm fine," she said, with a wave of her hand. "I'm just really tired."

"Of course you are. Come on. Let's get you upstairs."

"You don't have to come up. I don't need a nursemaid, you know."

He looked at her with a smile and asked, "How about just a friend?"

She stopped in her tracks, then turned to look at him, tears welling up in her eyes.

With a muffled exclamation, he walked closer and pulled her into his arms.

She sagged against him, as she held her. "I'm sorry," she muttered. "After everything you've done, I'm just being needy."

He chuckled. "No, you're just tired. I'm tired too. It's

been a long haul, but it ended well."

"That's what I have to remember," she said, as she tilted her head back and looked up at him, her tears still close to the surface. "I'm just … I think I'm just exhausted, and I should feel a whole lot better tomorrow."

"You will. Come on. Let's get you upstairs."

She didn't argue this time, as they headed inside the main building. "Do you know all your neighbors here? Do you have people to call on over the next few days?"

She shrugged and shook her head. "Honestly I've spent so much time tracking Frenchie with Johnny that I haven't really worried about getting to know any neighbors."

"Now might be a good time to reconnect with the living."

"No. I'm leaving. I've been thinking about it a lot over the last few days and had already made up my mind that, when this was all over with and I was done, I'm leaving. I'm heading out."

"Where to?"

She shrugged. "As much as I want to find a group like Terk's group, I don't think it's an open-door invitation, so maybe I'll head back to the US."

"*Back* to the US?" Radar asked.

She nodded. "I am here to grab a few things and to see if I can stay here or if my ex didn't destroy too much. If he did, I'll need a hotel for a few days. However, I need some clothes first. You brought the first lot, but I'm hoping I can get enough for a few days." She shrugged. "I spent a bunch of years here. Yet I don't really know many people, and I'm really too tired to even contemplate it."

"That makes the most sense."

When they got to her apartment door, he stepped back

to let her unlock it. Just as she went to turn the doorknob—and he would blame his delayed reaction on the fact that he too was exhausted—something slammed into his consciousness, and he grabbed her and threw her down the hallway, covering her quickly with his body, as the blast slammed through the building.

His head was filled with screams, and, as soon as the noise chilled, even with his ears ringing, he jumped to his feet, pashing back against the debris that had fallen on him. Picking her up in his arms, he raced to the far end of the hallway and out the back.

"Where are we going?" she mumbled, as she hung on tight.

"Out of here, somewhere safe."

"Is there such a thing?" she whispered.

"I hope so," he said in a consoling tone. "I really hope so." When they pushed through the building and finally into the fresh air, a shout came in his direction. Radar turned, and there was Riff, inside a vehicle.

"Get over here," he roared.

They raced toward him, and he helped them into the back seat. After that, Riff tore out of the parking lot.

"Did you know that would happen?" Radar asked.

"No," Riff admitted. "I just got this strange sense that I needed to come here. When I pulled into the lot, everything blew up. I had no idea where you were, then all of a sudden you came racing out the door."

Radar looked over at Sammy to confirm she was okay. She brushed his hands away. "I'm fine," she muttered, collapsing against his arms. "At least I think I am."

"Whatever that was, it's not something we were thinking about."

"No, and yet we should have been," she whispered. "If I wasn't so tired, I would have sensed it."

"And yet you didn't mention it."

"No, no, I didn't."

"Okay, so what's going on? You think this was just his last hurrah to make sure that he took you out at the same time? That would imply he knew who you were at the park."

"Yeah, he knew who I was at the park," she whispered, her eyes closed. "Nothing I could do about that. He's dead. How bad was the blast?"

"It didn't bring down the building. I'm not sure it hurt anybody other than your apartment and maybe the couple apartments next to it."

"I hope nobody else was hurt," she whispered.

"I hope so too," Riff agreed from the front seat, "but it's too early to know. Definitely a lot of help is on the way though."

"Maybe we should go back to assist them," she suggested, twisting around to look. But, out the back window, all they could see were emergency vehicles racing to the apartment building.

When his phone rang not even a moment later, Radar answered, "Yes, Terk. We're out. … Yeah, right? Thanks to Riff's timing, we're away from the scene. We're both okay, but I still want to get her checked over."

"I'm fine," she snapped, leaning into the phone. "I just wish I hadn't been so exhausted, or I would have seen that coming."

"All kinds of what-ifs happen in life," Terk noted, his voice calm. "Riff will bring you guys here."

"Really? Are you sure you want that?" Radar asked.

"Meaning?"

"It's just that … we could be bringing a lot of danger with us."

"That's fine," Terk replied. "Better we get to the bottom of it now."

"I suspect that whatever is happening is probably already over with," Radar shared, "but we'll have to wait for the bomb squad to confirm that."

"Do you really think we're out of danger?" she whispered. Just then they pulled up to a stop light. She looked around and in the vehicle beside them was an eerily familiar face. She pointed. "Look!" she cried out, as the vehicle pulled forward. She turned to Riff. "That vehicle, … go after him. That man, he looks life Frenchie but younger. That's got to be his son or a younger brother. He looks identical."

At that, Riff pulled into traffic and quickly headed after the vehicle.

"Are you sure?" Radar asked her. "You've just been through a hell of a shock."

"Yes, I have been," she stated bitterly, "but never did I realize there was a second relative, much less one close enough to pick up his battle."

"Maybe not even picking up the battle but ending it," Radar suggested.

When she realized he held her arm with a very fixed grip, she tried to pull away, then turned and glared at him. "What are you doing?"

He stared at her with a hard frown of his own. "I'm trying to stop the bleeding."

Staring at him for a moment, she then looked down at her arm, crying out softly, before slowly collapsing against him.

"How bad is it?" Riff inquired from the driver's seat.

"She's bleeding pretty heavily," Radar replied. "I've got pressure on it, and she'll hold for a little while, but, if I can't get it to slow down, we'll need a hospital and fast."

"We need to catch this guy."

"So keep going. Otherwise drop us off, and I'll catch a ride with her to the hospital."

At that, Riff snorted. "Like hell. I'm not dropping two injured people out in the middle of this nightmare." At that, the vehicle up ahead swerved and suddenly took a hard right. Riff almost caused an accident as he crossed traffic to go after it.

"This guy is pretty good," Radar noted, swearing slightly.

"Generally, when they come after us, they are," Riff muttered.

"You guys seem to have a way of making enemies," Radar noted.

"In this case, I think they're her enemies. Guess you better get on the phone and give Jonas the news."

"Will do."

At that, Radar picked up the phone. He wasn't able to get through, so he left Jonas a detailed message, telling him to call Terk for details. As soon as they were out on a clear stretch of highway, he noted the target vehicle speed up and weave through traffic. "Riff, with any luck, he will kill himself trying to get away."

"I'm not against that," Riff replied, as he followed carefully, his driving efficient and in control. "I just want to ensure we don't follow him down that path."

"Yeah, a wreck is not what we need to have happen at this point," Radar muttered. He looked at her arm and saw that the bleeding had slowed. "I think we're out of immediate danger with Sammy's bleeding here, but I don't know what else she might have for injuries."

"We'll get her checked out as soon as we get this guy," Riff stated.

Radar just didn't know what *getting this guy* would look like at the moment. As they raced through traffic, a semi came toward them, trundling along but at a reasonable speed. "Watch out for that guy."

"Oh, I can watch out for it," Riff confirmed, but, even as they watched, the speeding vehicle ahead swerved ever-so-slightly, lost control, and flipped in the air, slamming hard into the side of the semi, causing it to jackknife on the road.

Riff hit the brakes, squealing to a dead stop just before becoming part of the accident. Then Riff quickly pulled off to the shoulder, before other vehicles could slam into them.

Only silence followed.

CHAPTER 12

S AMMY OPENED HER eyes, hearing the sounds of sirens, more chaos, and voices shouting and screaming all around her. She struggled to come to full consciousness, only to hear a voice in her ear and to feel warm arms wrapped around her. "It's all right. Don't try to move. Just stay quiet."

She opened her eyes fully and stared up at Radar. "What the hell was that?" she murmured. "What happened?"

"Which part?" he asked, with a wry look. "Your apartment building blowing up, the high-speed car chase afterward, or the accident that the bomb maker's son caused?"

"Crap," she said, struggling to get up. Then realized she was still in the back of the vehicle. "God, I missed all that? What, was I asleep?"

"Unconscious, and it was probably for the best. Things got pretty harrowing there for a while."

She winced, and just then Riff came back over, opened up the vehicle, and looked in at her. "An ambulance is here. Let's make sure she gets in."

"No, I'm not going," she argued.

Riff just looked at her and replied, "I don't really care what you want. You're going." He looked over at Radar. "Are you taking her, or am I?"

She gripped Radar's arms and glared at Riff, who just laughed. Riff told her, "Believe me. After what Radar's just been through, I don't think he'll let you get away with skipping the hospital either."

At that, she looked up at Radar.

Radar nodded. "Riff's right. The bomb blast was bad enough, and, while Riff kept us out of the accident involving the semi, I've had a hell of a time getting your bleeding to slow down. So absolutely no way we won't at least get you checked over."

She sagged against him. "Fine, but can't you just drive me?"

Shaking his head, he said, "Look around, sweetheart." When she took a closer look and realized that, even if their vehicle was drivable, so much traffic was around them that they wouldn't get out of here for quite some time. The two of them helped her out of the vehicle, and by then she wasn't even protesting, perhaps not even able to. Several ambulances were on the scene, and she was quickly loaded into the back of one.

"I'll see you there," Radar told her firmly. She nodded. "Let the paramedics take care of you now."

As it was, she felt pretty woozy.

"Just lie back down," suggested one of them to her kindly, and, as soon as she did, her eyes closed, and she was out again.

WHEN SHE WOKE up the next time, she was in the hospital, tucked into a white bed in a bleached room. She groaned, feeling the pain kicking in hard.

"Take it easy," Radar muttered. "I'll get a nurse for you."

"No, no." She gasped, as she shifted. "I just need a moment to wake up."

"Is that all you need?" he asked, with a smile.

She glared at him. "How come you're not hurt?"

He shrugged. "Just lucky, I guess." Such cheerfulness filled his voice that she wondered if there was something she didn't know about. Then she asked, "Is it over now?"

"Thankfully, yes, it is over now. Although your apartment is pretty well destroyed, one of the bombs didn't go off, so the building itself might be salvageable. That will be up to the engineers, of course, but happily nobody else got hurt. Your apartment took the worst of the blast."

"That's something, at least," she said, with a heavy sigh. "I can't say I'm terribly impressed at losing everything though still things can be replaced."

"That's true, but, considering what you've been through, those are just things."

She smiled. "I agree. It was only a bunch of possessions, most that I didn't want anyway, especially if I'm moving."

"Yeah, look on the bright side," Radar noted, with a smile. "You have a whole lot less to move."

She would have laughed, but everything hurt. "So, how badly am I hurt?" she asked, looking down at her arm and chest. She wasn't able to get a good look at anything though.

"Lots of scratches and bruising, plus you've got a couple deeper cuts that needed a decent number of stitches," he admitted. "And, for that, I'm sorry."

She stared at him. "Sorry for what?"

"That I didn't catch the meaning or the message fast enough."

"You mean, your internal radar wasn't working?"

"Yeah," he replied, with a harsh look. "Apparently."

"You are human, and we were equally tired. Unfortunately it's the fatigue that likely took me out. I'm grateful that you weren't hurt."

He smiled. "I hear you there. I've also been …" Then he hesitated.

After a few moments of silence, she couldn't stand it. "You've also been … what?"

"According to Terk I have some serious skills that he wants to develop, if I'm interested."

Her eyes opened wide. "Wow, that is praise and deep."

"Not really," Radar replied. "According to him, and Gage told me this too, when you work together in a scenario like they have over there, the skills develop a little faster. So, while it might be difficult initially, he thinks I have the potential to improve quite a bit."

"But that would mean acknowledging that your internal radar is more than simply intuition," she noted, with a smirk.

"Yeah, I figured you would enjoy that," he admitted, with a sigh. "And it means working with a lot of people who probably have far more highly developed skills than I do."

"Ah, that could be quite challenging for you."

He smiled at her. "What about you? What will you do?"

"I don't know," she said. "I wasn't anticipating this stop on my journey, that's for sure." She snorted in disgust, as she looked around. "Presumably there's absolutely nothing left of my apartment, so I guess I'm footloose and fancy free."

He nodded. "I wondered … if you might want to … maybe spend a few days recuperating in a nicer location. Maybe pick up a little hotel or something on the seaside."

She frowned at him, yet a smile teased her lips. "Are you

suggesting it be just the two of us by any chance?"

"I was wondering about just the two of us," he admitted, with a growing smile. "Unless you feel the need to bring in reinforcements or something," he added, with an eye roll.

"No, I sure wasn't planning on that." Then she stopped and looked a bit alarmed. "What about Johnny? Is he still okay?"

"He and his family are in Amsterdam, and they're just fine," Radar shared calmly. "Their future will need a reboot as well, and he has already called several times to make sure you're okay. I've told him that you are, but, until you actually talk to him, he really won't believe me."

She smiled. "No, that's the thing about friends. You need to hear their voices."

"Exactly, so whenever you're feeling well enough, you can give him a quick call."

"That would imply that I had a phone."

At that, he pulled it from his pocket and placed it on the bedside table.

"Oh, I do have a phone," she shrieked, with a delighted smile. "Thank you for that."

"When you've lost quite a bit of your world already, somehow that phone makes a difference."

"It's everything in our world now, isn't it?" she muttered. A solemn look crossed her face, and she turned to him, looking serious.

"What is it?" he asked.

"Do we have any answers?"

"Some. That wasn't Frenchie's son. The team determined it was his nephew. Apparently the bomb maker was very close to this nephew, who apparently decided that, if his uncle didn't manage to make it all happen, he would be the last torch bearer and pull it off. Unfortunately he was killed in the car accident."

She nodded slowly, her shoulders slumping. "So, there won't be any answers, will there?"

"They'll still tear apart his life and get as many answers as they can, but realistically, with what you were able to confirm with the bomb maker in the park, it's pretty well *case closed* at this point."

She sighed, looked back out the window, and added, "I sure could have done without this last mess."

"Yes, but moving would be a lot more of a pain."

That forced out a chuckle. "Yeah. I don't even know where I'm going yet."

"Which is another good reason for taking some time to chill out at a nice quiet resort," he stated, with a smile. "Even if you don't want company, but maybe you should consider that."

"And if I do want company?"

"You only have to say the word."

She looked at him intently. "It's been a pretty rough road already."

"It has, and, if this isn't the kind of work you want to be involved in or even be involved with somebody who does this kind of work," he shared, with a shrug, "I'll be the first to understand."

"No, that's the thing. It seems to be what I need to do. I mean, I didn't have to jump on board and help Johnny either, but I did, and look where that ended up."

"Yeah, look where that ended up," he repeated, with a wry smile.

"We stopped a bomb maker from taking out who-knows-how-many-more people, and sure, I guess I didn't look quite deep enough into Frenchie's family, in order to protect myself a little more."

"That will be one of those lessons that you never quite let go of, I assume. Don't be surprised if it becomes one of those things that you always double and even triple-check now."

She smiled. "If not even more," she muttered. "By the way, the seaside sounds lovely."

He got up, moved closer to her bedside and said, "So, the seaside it is."

She burst out laughing. "What about the seaside holiday?"

"What?" he asked, obviously looking for clarification.

"Do you have a place in mind?" she asked curiously.

"I do," he declared. "Are you okay to leave it to me?"

She stared at him and then said, "I definitely can get behind that idea."

"It requires trust," he noted, with a warning.

"Yeah, well, … I think we're past that point, aren't we?"

"I am, but I still wanted to confirm that you were okay with it."

"I'm totally okay with it. You get me out of here, and I promise I'll be happy wherever we end up."

He burst out laughing. "That's hardly a good-enough answer, but I'll take it for now. Let me go talk to the doctors, and we'll see." And, with that, he got up and left.

She settled back, picked up her phone, and made some calls that needed to be done. Johnny was absolutely ecstatic to hear from her.

"It's so good to hear your voice. When I heard what happened, my heart just sank. I thought for sure it was over and when, … you know, … after all we'd been through."

"I'm fine, really. And now that you're reunited with your family, and you're all safe where you are, it's time to let this all go."

"Yeah, and you as well," he noted. "Although somehow I don't really see you letting Radar go."

"No, we'll go spend a week at a seaside resort apparently, so I have some time to recuperate. Which is good, since it's not as if I have any place to move to now," she stated in a wry tone.

"Did you have insurance?"

"I might have, but, of course, all my records were in the apartment too."

"But there are such things as computer records, and I'm sure you can sort it all out."

She laughed. "I'm pretty sure I can track down what I need to track down online on my own."

At that, Johnny burst out laughing. "I would think so, given that's what we do, and you do it so well that you might want to consider continuing along that line."

"I have considered it. I'm just not sure which avenue I want to travel in," she shared. "I can do the work, but I need a break."

"We all do," Johnny stated, true caring evident in his voice. "And speaking of that, I'll go take my kids and my wife to the park and enjoy just being alive, forgetting about what we've recently been through. You take care of yourself."

She smiled and was still smiling when Radar walked back in, pushing a wheelchair. She stared at the wheelchair, asking, "What's this for? More tests?"

He chuckled. "No, I'm breaking you out of here."

She stared at him in shock for a moment, then threw back the covers and hopped up. Almost immediately the room swam around in circles, and she gave a hoarse shout.

Radar raced to her side and caught her before she hit the floor. "Now that," he said, settling her in the wheelchair, "was one of the dumbest moves I've seen you make."

She groaned. "Don't make me laugh," she whispered. "I already hurt."

He smiled and nodded. "How about a trip to the bathroom? I'm sorry. I should have gotten you some clothes, but I didn't think that far ahead."

"That's fine. We can buy what we need either on the way or there."

"I'll find a place," he said, and, before long, they were outside, and she was slowly getting into a vehicle. When she noted Riff standing there, she smiled at him. "Thank you."

He nodded. "Not sure what for, but I'll take it."

She snorted. "I probably don't even have a clue about what you've done for me, all of you," she began, "so just pass along that I'm grateful to have my life. Even though it's a bit of a mess at the moment, I hope you are happy with whatever demons you're left dealing with."

"Happy with whatever demons?" he asked, then he stared at her intently. "You hunt people, don't you?"

"Yes, I do. Why?"

"Because I might have somebody I need you to help hunt for me."

She nodded. "We can talk, after I get some downtime and a chance to recover for a few days."

"I heard you're heading to a seaside resort," Riff added, with a smirk.

"Apparently, although I'm not sure where it might be."

"Don't worry about it," Radar said, as he got into the driver's seat. "You'll find out soon enough."

She turned to Riff, as Radar started up the engine. "We'll talk afterward."

Riff nodded. "Take care of yourself and enjoy. You'll need the rest."

"I'll need the rest?" she repeated, her eyebrows raising. "Why?"

He gave her a knowing smile. "We'll see you later." And, with that, he turned and walked away.

"Does he have wheels? Does he need anything?" she asked. "He's one of the strangest men who I've ever met."

"He is," Radar agreed, "but he's on our side, and, for that, I am grateful."

"Yeah, you're not kidding," she muttered.

CHAPTER 13

S AMMY WOKE UP several mornings later and smiled at the beautiful sunshine that poured in through the double glass doors. The soft rays danced across her sheets. When she heard a knock, she looked over and smiled as Radar walked in, carrying a tray. She sat up in bed, wincing at the residual soreness.

"How're you doing?" he asked, catching the grimace on her face.

She snorted. "I'm fine. I think it's just more reflexive than anything." He nodded and settled the tray on her lap. She noted two cups of coffee. "This is a habit I can get into."

"What? Coffee delivered in the morning?" he asked, with a teasing note.

"That and your smiling face," she admitted.

He froze in the act of straightening up, then looked over at her and asked, "Really?"

She smiled. "Besides, you found this absolutely luxurious place on the French Riviera, when I didn't even think something like this was available to rent." They were to stay for a week in this beautiful little cottage with a view and privacy, surrounded by trees, plus a full kitchen, along with restaurants and other amenities within walking distance. "This is absolutely gorgeous, and I can't imagine how you found it."

"Through a friend of a friend," he said, with a nonchalant smile. "Besides, I figured we needed the time."

She nodded. "What about you?" she asked, looking up at him. "How are you doing?"

"Rested," he declared, with a dimpled smile, as he climbed up gently onto the bed and sat beside her, leaning against the headboard.

She looked over and patted his cheek. "You're looking better. Your skin is glowing again, and your eyes don't have the exhaustion."

"Hey," he quipped, pulling back ever-so-slightly, "that's hardly what I need to hear."

"Okay then, that devil-may-care grin has returned and that rakish look is back in your gaze."

His eyes widened at that, and he chuckled. "That sounds much better."

She burst out laughing and shifted ever-so-slightly, moving gently to not dislodge the tray, then picked up one of the two cups. "Here you go," she said.

"Any decision yet on your future?"

"No, … none," she replied, with a happy sigh, as she settled back in and closed her eyes, turning her face into the sunlight. "Maybe that's just what I need to do. Make no decisions for a while."

"Sounds good to me," he agreed, taking a sip of his coffee, as the two of them shared a few moments of peace and gentleness between them. "Any particular plans for the day?" he asked. "What appeals?"

She shifted her arm experimentally. "The arm is doing pretty well. Maybe we can change the dressing after this."

"Yeah, and we probably need to get the stitches taken out in a few days."

She pondered that. "I think he said ten days, didn't he?"

"Probably, and it's certainly not that time yet."

"No, I hear you," she replied, as she finished her coffee, then shifted the tray to the side table, so she could get up. She walked into the bathroom, quickly washed her face, and straightened out her hair. By the time she came back out, he'd stretched out on the bed, just staring up at the ceiling, his hands resting under his head. She clambered up onto the bed to sit beside him. "What do you want to do today?" she asked.

He rolled his head toward her, then winked at her suggestively.

She flushed. "Oh, I see. So, in other words, wandering the beach half-nude in our bathing suits and just sitting outside and enjoying life."

"A little more than that too, maybe, … if you're fully rested," he added, looking at her with a twinkling gaze. "I've been trying so hard not to push it."

"I noticed," she admitted, studying him, now on one elbow at his side. "Can't say it's the most romantic moment though."

At that, he gently knocked her arm out from under her, sending her tumbling onto his chest. "I don't know about that. I've been trying very hard to not rush, giving your body time to heal."

She smiled. "I think my body is just fine."

"Are you sure about that?" he murmured, as he tilted up her chin and assessed her gaze, his thumb gently stroking her bottom lip.

"I am," she declared. "I also got an interesting text."

"Oh? From whom?"

"Terk," she said. Radar nodded, as if it were no surprise.

"You told Terk about me, didn't you?"

He looked up at her and laughed. "That's the thing about Terk. Nobody ever has to tell him anything. He already knew about you." When she frowned at that, he ticked the corner of her mouth with his thumb and said, "No frowning. … So, what do you think of his offer?"

"Ah, so he told you?" she asked him.

"No, but he wouldn't have contacted you otherwise."

"I don't know whether that's true or not because I don't know him well enough, but he did suggest that I spend some time over there, as if to say that maybe I had something to offer. He didn't offer me a job necessarily, but told me that I was welcome to come and spend time there."

"What do you think of that?"

"I think it's a hell of an offer," she admitted, "and I would be a fool to say no."

"Good. I'm glad to hear that. I didn't want you to come just because of me, but I was hoping that, if something were to open up, you would want to."

"It's not as if I have anything else on my plate at the moment," she noted.

"Just me," he pointed out, "and I'll take an awful lot of looking after."

She burst out laughing. "Oh, I see. So, you bring me coffee in the morning and look after me while I'm injured, not to mention bringing me to the French Riviera to rest up, and now, all of a sudden, I'm indebted to looking after you?"

"Yeah, that sounds about right," he agreed, with a nod. "Of course, a few other things are in there, like the fact that we work well together and that we obviously have some energy connection together, which you were all about, until suddenly you backed off."

"No, I didn't back off," she corrected with a sigh, as she reached up her arms and stretched across his chest. "I think life just got in the way."

"I'll accept that too. It has been a pretty strange couple of weeks."

"It has," she murmured. "On the other hand, we made it, and now we're on the other side of all that chaos."

"Are you sure you're ready to get back into that again?" he asked. "Terk's place may not be much calmer."

"Yet I'm not sure how much actual fieldwork I would have to do, compared to the computer work."

"That's important too, and it's one of the questions I have for him as well, since I would be looking to do fieldwork."

"I'm okay with you doing fieldwork, as long as you come home," she stated, her tone very serious.

At that, his gaze turned smoky. "Yeah? Is there a particular reason you want me to come home?"

She flushed, then, quickly gathering her determination, she leaned over and kissed him on the lips. "I've got a lot of reasons, but the biggest one is that I care and that I like having you right here with me. There is definitely something between us, and I really want to see where that goes."

"I thought that's why we're here," he teased in mock confusion.

She grinned at him. "Ha, ha. We could just be here to enjoy some time together, with absolutely no permanence as to our future."

"I'm all about permanence," he declared. "I waited a long time to find somebody. We could be a matched set."

"Wow, I like that." She stared at him. "And here I thought you weren't the romantic kind."

"I'm not sure I'm the romantic kind that most women like so much, but I definitely have some sense of romance in my soul," he protested.

"You don't need much," she indicated. "I would take sincerity over anything else any day."

"That is something I have in spades."

She nodded, then reached up and kissed him again. "So, what do I tell Terk?"

"What do you want to tell him?"

"I don't know," she muttered. "I've been thinking about it since I heard you worked for him. Obviously I want to come, but …"

"What?" he asked, in exasperation. "Spit it out."

She laughed. "Do I tell him about us?"

"You don't have to tell Terk about us," he replied.

She looked at him surprise. "Oh, so you did already?" Her mind was overwhelmed with that.

"No. See? That's the thing about Terk that you still don't get. You don't have to tell him stuff. He already knows, and the fact that he has invited you there, it means he already knows about us."

"Do you think so?"

"Oh, I know so," he said, sliding his hands up to her shoulders, gently massaging the back of her neck. "I can guarantee he already knows."

"You think he's okay with it?"

"I think that, in his world, we come as matched sets, and, when he brings one, he knows the other is coming too. I haven't met the whole team yet, so I can't be sure, but I think some sort of a bond forms. So he has to ensure the energy will gel with everybody else on the team."

She propped her head up on her hands across his chest,

then smiled at him. "Meaning, we've been given the seal of approval, and he thinks it will work out well."

"I think so. Although I'm not even sure how well *we'll* work out yet," he noted, then waggled his eyebrows.

She burst out laughing. "So, well, … we could find out right now." She leaned forward and kissed him softly, teasing him, but that kiss ended up getting her gently flipped onto her back, then a warm body slid atop her. As he deepened the kiss, his tongue slid in behind her lips to duel gently with her own. When he finally lifted his head, she was almost cross-eyed.

"Wow," she muttered. "If I'd known that was waiting for me—"

"It was always waiting for you," he stated, "right from the time we met, and you knew it."

"I did know it," she muttered. "Yet I had a hard time acknowledging it. And, when I finally did, it seemed you had no clue."

"Sometimes it's like that," he admitted, as he lowered his head and kissed her gently on the cheek, on her forehead, on her nose. "But the thing is, we have time. We have time to get to know each other, and we have time to love each other. We have a whole future ahead of us." Then he lowered his head again and kissed her deeply, again and again. When he finally came up for air, she breathed heavily underneath him.

She smiled up at him. "So, I guess I have an idea of what we can do."

"Yeah, what's that?" he muttered, as he trailed kisses down her neck and across her shoulders.

She breathed heavily against his ear and whispered, "This." She kissed him, this time her hand sliding down between them to the hard proof of his own emotions, sliding her hand around his shaft and moving gently up and down.

He shuddered against her, his hips already pulsing. "Man, I can't think of anything I want to do more."

She chuckled again, only to find he was up, tossing his clothes left and right, as he stripped down in front of her. When he stood proudly in front of her, she reached out with both hands, but he chuckled and motioned at her nightie. "That's got to go."

She rolled her eyes and said, "But it's hardly anything."

"It's got to go," he muttered.

And, with that, she slipped it over her head. With her arms still trapped up top, he gently pinned them above her head, then chuckling, lowered her onto her back, where he kissed her and again and then again. He slowly worked his way down, taking one plump breast in his hand and laved the nipple with his tongue. Then he gave the same ministration to the other one, as she twisted beneath him.

"Holy crap," she muttered.

He moved up her body to face her, then smiled and said, "Remember that energy stuff?"

"What energy stuff?" she asked, gasping as his hand slid over her hip and along her thigh to gently caress her knee and then come back up underneath. "Christ." She slid her hand through his hair. "What energy?"

He explained, "Just think about the energy you use when you're hunting."

"Yeah, what about it?"

"Start it up."

She stared at him and frowned. "Is it something we can start and stop?" Almost immediately she saw a probe coming toward her. She gasped in delight, as she opened up her senses to meet it head-on. "Oh my," she gasped, as their energies twisted and turned together. She wrapped her arms around him, pulling them up close. "Is that us?"

"Absolutely it's us," Radar confirmed. "Some of what we have coming toward us."

"I could get behind that," she murmured, as she twisted beneath him, her thighs widening and wrapping around him, as she surged upward, while sending him a huge pulse of energy.

He groaned as it slammed into him and went right to his groin. He plunged deep within her. Then he started to move, their movements almost frantic with need, as they strove to the end, before climaxing together and crashing back down on the waves of pure sexual energy fueled by love—and their twin energies.

She sighed against his mouth. "Definitely staying here and doing this all day."

He chuckled against her, slid slowly off to the side, but kept her close and whispered, "Sounds perfect."

"Just like you are," she muttered gently. He shook his head, but she placed a finger against his lips. "Don't argue," she ordered.

He burst out laughing. "Okay, I'll try not to." But he rolled his eyes at her.

She smiled. "I love that we can have fun with each other."

"That is definitely a benefit," he murmured. "Still, it was important to know that we would blend on more than just one level."

"I don't think this energy can be wrong, can it?"

"I hope not," he said. "I want to think that we have a special place that is perfect and just for us."

"Then again," she added, "I'm also a believer in what we

can create. So, as far as I'm concerned, … that becomes our future."

He nodded. "In that case," he murmured, as he rolled atop her again, "how about we work on that *all day long.*"

"Sounds good to me," she whispered, as she pulled him to her again. "Then I think we should talk to Terk."

"You can talk to him. Call him if you want," he murmured. "However, I can tell you that he already knows what you'll say." He lifted his head, grinned at her, and added, "So do I for that matter."

"Yeah, and what will I say?"

"You'll say, 'Thanks, Terk. I would love to come. I was planning on coming anyway. I just hadn't told Radar yet.'"

She burst out laughing and then looked at him seriously. "How did you know?"

"I could feel it," he admitted. "You assumed I haven't been aware of this energy between us, but it's just been a matter of trying to figure out how important and how dedicated we were to it."

"Oh, I think we're pretty dedicated," she quipped, with a chuckle. She lifted her hips against him. "So this Terk talk can be done later," she whispered, feeling the same urgency rising within. "Right now it's just us."

"That sounds perfect." Radar lowered his head and kissed her again.

T ERK SAT AT the massive table, but the team was already trying to figure out how much bigger to make this seating arrangement. Terk stared at the table. "Can you imagine that we even thought we would need something this size? There's already, what? Sixteen of us?"

"That's not something I thought would happen," Gage replied. "At least not so soon."

"Right." Terk smiled. "The thing is, we've done very well."

"What about Radar?"

"Well, … Radar will be coming on when he's ready. He needs a bit of training," Terk noted, "but that will be true for anybody who isn't on our team already."

"Right. So we'll need to potentially have somebody else coming on board to help out. What about Riff?"

"Riff is a world unto himself," Terk noted. "He did a great job helping out and being in the right spot at the right time."

"What about the woman who called you. Did she call back?"

"The sister to Riff's dead fiancée? She only phoned once," he said. "And I suspect she'll be here soon enough, whether we like it or not."

"Her energy is strong, isn't it?"

"Absolutely, but when she does get here, she'll be a force we'll have to deal with."

"And dealing with her won't be easy, especially if she's set on helping Riff with his problem."

"Riff will be in and out, at least for the next little while anyway," Terk shared. "He's got a lead on something, but he'll be back. So, if we need him on the next job, we just have to tag him, and he'll show up."

"He seems to do that a lot, doesn't he? Come and go, I mean."

"It's part of who he is, but, at the same time, he's somebody we desperately need to call on when we have problems."

"What about the billing aspect of this first MI6 job?" Celia asked, as she joined Terk at the table. "What did Jonas do with that?"

"Not only did we get a bonus for saving the government agents but, because of the double bombings and the other aspects that went into it that were outside the scope of the original assignment, our expenses are completely covered. Plus we got an extra 17 percent on top of all that, according to the calculations I worked out. They didn't even quibble," Terk added.

"Does that make you wonder if you've charged enough?" she asked in a teasing voice.

"Of course it does." He gave his wife a smirk. "I tossed it back and forth with Ice, and she confirmed that it was a really nicely paid job and to ensure we do everything we can to keep MI6 in our pocket because that level of job doesn't come by all the time."

"No, and that'll be something we want to encourage then," Celia noted, "because we're running through the cash pretty quickly, especially if we're saving for our own satellite."

"That is an understatement," Terk replied. "As we start trying to get some of these higher-level things in place, we'll need to set up an ongoing budget."

"Exactly, and there'll be an awful lot of people here, depending on the time frame that's needed just to get that satellite."

"Also"—Terk eyed the twin sisters with their special healing abilities heading toward the big dining table—"when Sammy gets here, she's been injured."

At that, both sisters nodded. "Yes, we've already been working on those injuries," Cara shared. "That deepest cut is pretty well healed and should be good to go. With this many people going back and forth all the time, our energies could get split up pretty easily."

"You can't wear yourselves down either," Terk warned, looking at them quite sternly.

They just smiled. Clary replied, "You also know that healing others helps us heal ourselves, so that's not really anything to worry about."

"Maybe not," he conceded, "but apparently I'm worrying enough for all of you." He pointed at their obviously pregnant states.

The twins burst out laughing at that. "Maybe," Cara admitted, "but who knew you would be such a worrisome dad."

"I didn't even think I could be," Terk admitted, with a headshake. "Yet this whole scenario has absolutely blown me away."

"All of us actually," Celia noted, with a gentle smile for her husband. "But, as long as we don't have any other jobs at the moment, we should be good."

Just then Terk's phone rang. He looked down at it and frowned. "Terk here." The voice at the other end was one he knew but from a long time ago. "Jeremy, what the hell?" At the sound of an old friend, Terk smiled into the phone. "What's up? … What do you mean?" he asked, listening to Jeremy ramble. "Hang on, hang on. Let me put this on Speakerphone, so the rest of the team can hear."

"You have a team?" Jeremy asked, with audible relief. "I heard you were done with the CIA."

"Yeah, but we've set up in the private sector."

"Thank God for that," he said. "As you well know, I'm still in the damn black ops business, but two of our teams have been taken, and we need you to do a reconnaissance mission. I'm presuming you can still stay where you are for that."

"I don't know whether we can or not. You'll have to give us a whole lot more information than that. And, if we have to send somebody, we'll send somebody. I do have some available people on our team who could go," he added, yet frowning as he looked around at everybody.

"I have one man in particular I need to bring back," Jeremy stated, "but he's injured, and I can tell you that he's damn good at what he does, but he took a blast, and I'm not sure what kind of … it's somebody you know."

"Yeah, who's that?"

"Legend. He was kidnapped and beaten, but he escaped. The last we heard, he was attacked, and, after that, we lost contact. We don't know whether he's alive or dead."

"Holy shit." Terk pinched the bridge of his nose. "He was unparalleled in his field."

"Yeah, and he has some of that weird stuff that you do,

but we've had no communication from him. So, if you have any way of tracking where he is, just give us a location, so we can retrieve him. I really want to get him back again."

"Why is that?" Terk asked, hating the suspicion evident in his tone. "We will likely need to be involved."

Jeremy frowned and then said, "You might as well know it all. We're wondering if he was involved right from the beginning. As in for the wrong side. Others are grumbling about treason, and I don't want to believe it, but …"

"Absolutely no way," Terk declared.

"Good," Jeremy replied, "then prove it. We're hiring you and your team to get him and maybe, if needed, to prove that he's innocent because otherwise, as far as we can tell, that best friend of yours is guilty as hell."

This concludes Book 1 of Terk's Guardians: Radar.
Read about Legend: Terk's Guardians, Book 2

Terk's Guardians: Legend (Book #2)

When Legend sees his political war-mongering father heading in a direction Legend can't agree with, he walks, but walking away from his little brother, Larry, can't happen. He is special in so many ways—even Clary, who has helped him many times, agrees. When intel of a government uprising is confirmed, Legend swoops in to remove Larry from the danger zone. It's not like Legend can leave behind his brother's tutor either ...

Blair has been looking after Larry for years and had expected her position to continue for much longer, but, when Legend races in, barking orders to leave, her calm future is in sudden jeopardy. Nothing is easy or calm about Legend when he's around her.

As the coup fails, Legend's simple escape plan deteriorates quickly, and Larry's existence is suddenly a prize for cohorts, who haven't been paid and who are looking for a quick escape route too. Not that Blair would let anyone hurt her charge—even if it means dealing with and cooperating with the very irritating Legend.

Find Book 2 here!

To find out more visit Dale Mayer's website.

https://geni.us/DMSLegend

Author's Note

Thank you for reading Radar: Terk's Guardians, Book 1! If you enjoyed the book, please take a moment and leave a short review.

Dear reader,

I love to hear from readers, and you can contact me at my website: www.dalemayer.com or at my Facebook author page. To be informed of new releases and special offers, sign up for my newsletter or follow me on BookBub. And if you are interested in joining Dale Mayer's Reader Group, here is the Facebook sign up page.
http://geni.us/DaleMayerFBGroup

Cheers,
Dale Mayer

About the Author

Dale Mayer is a *USA Today* best-selling author, best known for her SEALs military romances, her Psychic Visions series, and her Lovely Lethal Garden cozy series. Her contemporary romances are raw and full of passion and emotion (Broken But … Mending, Hathaway House series). Her thrillers will keep you guessing (Kate Morgan, By Death series), and her romantic comedies will keep you giggling (*It's a Dog's Life*, a stand-alone novella; and the Broken Protocols series, starring Charming Marvin, the cat).

Dale honors the stories that come to her—and some of them are crazy, break all the rules and cross multiple genres!

To go with her fiction, she also writes nonfiction in many different fields, with books available on résumé writing, companion gardening, and the US mortgage system. All her books are available in print and ebook format.

Connect with Dale Mayer Online

Dale's Website – www.dalemayer.com
Twitter – @DaleMayer
Facebook Page – geni.us/DaleMayerFBFanPage
Facebook Group – geni.us/DaleMayerFBGroup
BookBub – geni.us/DaleMayerBookbub
Instagram – geni.us/DaleMayerInstagram
Goodreads – geni.us/DaleMayerGoodreads
Newsletter – geni.us/DaleNews

Also by Dale Mayer

Published Adult Books:

Shadow Recon
Magnus, Book 1
Rogan, Book 2
Egan, Book 3
Barret, Book 4

Bullard's Battle
Ryland's Reach, Book 1
Cain's Cross, Book 2
Eton's Escape, Book 3
Garret's Gambit, Book 4
Kano's Keep, Book 5
Fallon's Flaw, Book 6
Quinn's Quest, Book 7
Bullard's Beauty, Book 8
Bullard's Best, Book 9
Bullard's Battle, Books 1–2
Bullard's Battle, Books 3–4
Bullard's Battle, Books 5–6
Bullard's Battle, Books 7–8

Terkel's Team
Damon's Deal, Book 1
Wade's War, Book 2

Gage's Goal, Book 3
Calum's Contact, Book 4
Rick's Road, Book 5
Scott's Summit, Book 6
Brody's Beast, Book 7
Terkel's Twist, Book 8
Terkel's Triumph, Book 9

Terk's Guardians
Radar, Book 1
Legend, Book 2

Kate Morgan
Simon Says… Hide, Book 1
Simon Says… Jump, Book 2
Simon Says… Ride, Book 3
Simon Says… Scream, Book 4
Simon Says… Run, Book 5
Simon Says… Walk, Book 6
Simon Says… Forgive, Book 7

Hathaway House
Aaron, Book 1
Brock, Book 2
Cole, Book 3
Denton, Book 4
Elliot, Book 5
Finn, Book 6
Gregory, Book 7
Heath, Book 8
Iain, Book 9
Jaden, Book 10

Keith, Book 11
Lance, Book 12
Melissa, Book 13
Nash, Book 14
Owen, Book 15
Percy, Book 16
Quinton, Book 17
Ryatt, Book 18
Spencer, Book 19
Timothy, Book 20
Urban, Book 21
Hathaway House, Books 1–3
Hathaway House, Books 4–6
Hathaway House, Books 7–9

The K9 Files

Ethan, Book 1
Pierce, Book 2
Zane, Book 3
Blaze, Book 4
Lucas, Book 5
Parker, Book 6
Carter, Book 7
Weston, Book 8
Greyson, Book 9
Rowan, Book 10
Caleb, Book 11
Kurt, Book 12
Tucker, Book 13
Harley, Book 14
Kyron, Book 15
Jenner, Book 16

Rhys, Book 17
Landon, Book 18
Harper, Book 19
Kascius, Book 20
Declan, Book 21
The K9 Files, Books 1–2
The K9 Files, Books 3–4
The K9 Files, Books 5–6
The K9 Files, Books 7–8
The K9 Files, Books 9–10
The K9 Files, Books 11–12

Lovely Lethal Gardens

Arsenic in the Azaleas, Book 1
Bones in the Begonias, Book 2
Corpse in the Carnations, Book 3
Daggers in the Dahlias, Book 4
Evidence in the Echinacea, Book 5
Footprints in the Ferns, Book 6
Gun in the Gardenias, Book 7
Handcuffs in the Heather, Book 8
Ice Pick in the Ivy, Book 9
Jewels in the Juniper, Book 10
Killer in the Kiwis, Book 11
Lifeless in the Lilies, Book 12
Murder in the Marigolds, Book 13
Nabbed in the Nasturtiums, Book 14
Offed in the Orchids, Book 15
Poison in the Pansies, Book 16
Quarry in the Quince, Book 17
Revenge in the Roses, Book 18
Silenced in the Sunflowers, Book 19

Toes up in the Tulips, Book 20
Uzi in the Urn, Book 21
Victim in the Violets, Book 22
Lovely Lethal Gardens, Books 1–2
Lovely Lethal Gardens, Books 3–4
Lovely Lethal Gardens, Books 5–6
Lovely Lethal Gardens, Books 7–8
Lovely Lethal Gardens, Books 9–10

Psychic Visions Series

Tuesday's Child
Hide 'n Go Seek
Maddy's Floor
Garden of Sorrow
Knock Knock…
Rare Find
Eyes to the Soul
Now You See Her
Shattered
Into the Abyss
Seeds of Malice
Eye of the Falcon
Itsy-Bitsy Spider
Unmasked
Deep Beneath
From the Ashes
Stroke of Death
Ice Maiden
Snap, Crackle…
What If…
Talking Bones
String of Tears

Inked Forever
Insanity
Psychic Visions Books 1–3
Psychic Visions Books 4–6
Psychic Visions Books 7–9

By Death Series
Touched by Death
Haunted by Death
Chilled by Death
By Death Books 1–3

Broken Protocols – Romantic Comedy Series
Cat's Meow
Cat's Pajamas
Cat's Cradle
Cat's Claus
Broken Protocols 1-4

Broken and... Mending
Skin
Scars
Scales (of Justice)
Broken but... Mending 1-3

Glory
Genesis
Tori
Celeste
Glory Trilogy

Biker Blues
Morgan: Biker Blues, Volume 1

Cash: Biker Blues, Volume 2

SEALs of Honor

Mason: SEALs of Honor, Book 1

Hawk: SEALs of Honor, Book 2

Dane: SEALs of Honor, Book 3

Swede: SEALs of Honor, Book 4

Shadow: SEALs of Honor, Book 5

Cooper: SEALs of Honor, Book 6

Markus: SEALs of Honor, Book 7

Evan: SEALs of Honor, Book 8

Mason's Wish: SEALs of Honor, Book 9

Chase: SEALs of Honor, Book 10

Brett: SEALs of Honor, Book 11

Devlin: SEALs of Honor, Book 12

Easton: SEALs of Honor, Book 13

Ryder: SEALs of Honor, Book 14

Macklin: SEALs of Honor, Book 15

Corey: SEALs of Honor, Book 16

Warrick: SEALs of Honor, Book 17

Tanner: SEALs of Honor, Book 18

Jackson: SEALs of Honor, Book 19

Kanen: SEALs of Honor, Book 20

Nelson: SEALs of Honor, Book 21

Taylor: SEALs of Honor, Book 22

Colton: SEALs of Honor, Book 23

Troy: SEALs of Honor, Book 24

Axel: SEALs of Honor, Book 25

Baylor: SEALs of Honor, Book 26

Hudson: SEALs of Honor, Book 27

Lachlan: SEALs of Honor, Book 28

Paxton: SEALs of Honor, Book 29

Bronson: SEALs of Honor, Book 30

Hale: SEALs of Honor, Book 31

SEALs of Honor, Books 1–3

SEALs of Honor, Books 4–6

SEALs of Honor, Books 7–10

SEALs of Honor, Books 11–13

SEALs of Honor, Books 14–16

SEALs of Honor, Books 17–19

SEALs of Honor, Books 20–22

SEALs of Honor, Books 23–25

Heroes for Hire

Levi's Legend: Heroes for Hire, Book 1

Stone's Surrender: Heroes for Hire, Book 2

Merk's Mistake: Heroes for Hire, Book 3

Rhodes's Reward: Heroes for Hire, Book 4

Flynn's Firecracker: Heroes for Hire, Book 5

Logan's Light: Heroes for Hire, Book 6

Harrison's Heart: Heroes for Hire, Book 7

Saul's Sweetheart: Heroes for Hire, Book 8

Dakota's Delight: Heroes for Hire, Book 9

Tyson's Treasure: Heroes for Hire, Book 10

Jace's Jewel: Heroes for Hire, Book 11

Rory's Rose: Heroes for Hire, Book 12

Brandon's Bliss: Heroes for Hire, Book 13

Liam's Lily: Heroes for Hire, Book 14

North's Nikki: Heroes for Hire, Book 15

Anders's Angel: Heroes for Hire, Book 16

Reyes's Raina: Heroes for Hire, Book 17

Dezi's Diamond: Heroes for Hire, Book 18

Vince's Vixen: Heroes for Hire, Book 19

Ice's Icing: Heroes for Hire, Book 20

SEALs of Steel

The Mavericks

Kerrick, Book 1
Griffin, Book 2
Jax, Book 3
Beau, Book 4
Asher, Book 5
Ryker, Book 6
Miles, Book 7
Nico, Book 8
Keane, Book 9
Lennox, Book 10
Gavin, Book 11
Shane, Book 12
Diesel, Book 13
Jerricho, Book 14
Killian, Book 15
Hatch, Book 16
Corbin, Book 17
Aiden, Book 18
The Mavericks, Books 1–2
The Mavericks, Books 3–4
The Mavericks, Books 5–6
The Mavericks, Books 7–8
The Mavericks, Books 9–10
The Mavericks, Books 11–12

Standalone Novellas

It's a Dog's Life
Riana's Revenge
Second Chances

Published Young Adult Books:

Family Blood Ties Series

Vampire in Denial

Vampire in Distress

Vampire in Design

Vampire in Deceit

Vampire in Defiance

Vampire in Conflict

Vampire in Chaos

Vampire in Crisis

Vampire in Control

Vampire in Charge

Family Blood Ties Set 1–3

Family Blood Ties Set 1–5

Family Blood Ties Set 4–6

Family Blood Ties Set 7–9

Sian's Solution, A Family Blood Ties Series Prequel
Novelette

Design series

Dangerous Designs

Deadly Designs

Darkest Designs

Design Series Trilogy

Standalone

In Cassie's Corner

Gem Stone (a Gemma Stone Mystery)

Time Thieves

Published Non-Fiction Books:

Career Essentials

Career Essentials: The Résumé
Career Essentials: The Cover Letter
Career Essentials: The Interview
Career Essentials: 3 in 1

48294CB00002B/591

www.ingramcontent.com/pod-product-compliance
Lightning Source LLC
Chambersburg PA
CBHW071431200726